This book may be kept 14 days.

A fine of 5 cents per day will be charged on books kept overtime.

No books will be issued to persons in arrear for fines.

Books must not be loaned by the borrower.

Careful usage of books is expected, and any soiling, injury, or loss is to be paid for by the borrower.

GINNIE AND THE MYSTERY DOLL

Other Books by Catherine Woolley

THE ANIMAL TRAIN

DAVID'S CAMPAIGN BUTTONS

DAVID'S HUNDRED DOLLARS

DAVID'S RAILROAD

ELLIE'S PROBLEM DOG

GINNIE AND GENEVA

GINNIE AND THE MYSTERY HOUSE

GINNIE AND THE NEW GIRL

GINNIE JOINS IN

HOLIDAY ON WHEELS

LUNCH FOR LENNIE

MISS CATHY LEONARD

RAILROAD COWBOY

A ROOM FOR CATHY

SCHOOLROOM ZOO

TWO HUNDRED PENNIES

GINNIE
AND
THE MYSTERY DOLL

By Catherine Woolley

Illustrated by Patricia Boodell

WILLIAM MORROW AND COMPANY

New York, 1960

CONTENTS

GINNIE AND THE MYSTERY DOLL

CHAPTER 1

The House on the Cape

ON the Mid-Cape Highway the cloudless July sky had arched, blue and dazzling gold, over lakes and woods. But the old town lay in cool shadow, its houses white beneath riots of rambler roses, as Mr. Fellows brought the car to a halt in front of the post office.

Ginnie, in the back seat, sat up straight and uttered a sigh of relief. "I thought we'd never get here!"

Beside her Geneva gave an excited wriggle. "It seems like two years since we left home!" Honey, the blond cocker, panted with interest.

Actually they had left home that morning, so early that they had been ready for lunch by ten-thirty. It was hard to believe, Ginnie thought, that it was only two o'clock now.

"Where's my mother and father?" Geneva demanded, twisting to look out the back window.

"Right beside us," Ginnie's mother said, as the Porter car, which had followed them all the way from New Jersey, pulled up to park.

"Come on, Ginnie, let's get out," Geneva cried impatiently.

This was the start of the wonderful holiday that both girls had been talking and thinking about since early spring, when the two families had decided to take a summer house together on Cape Cod.

"Just a minute, you two," Daddy said. "I'll let you out. What's the name of this agent I'm supposed to call?"

"Her name is Evans," Mother told him. "Mrs. Evans. Here's her phone number."

Daddy went to the public telephone booth outside the post office and Mr. Porter got out of his car. Ginnie followed her father to the booth. "I hope she's home."

He dropped a dime in the slot and dialed.

"She'll be home. They said the house would be ready after two o'clock. Hello!" He spoke into the phone. "Mrs. Evans? This is Mr. Fellows. We're over at the post office. Right! Thank you." He hung up. "She'll be down to take us to the house."

Ginnie galloped back to the car. "She's coming!"

The girls and their fathers went into a little store. It was dim and cool and smelled of packaged cakes and the fresh print of the latest magazines, which crowded the racks. They bought ice cream to eat while they waited. Ginnie was licking off the last bit of chocolate coating when a shabby black coupé drew up beside the Fellows car.

The woman at the wheel leaned out. "Mr. Fellows? How do you do? If you'll follow me I'll take you to the house."

So they were off again, following Mrs. Evans down the sunny highway, turning soon into a narrower road that dipped into young woods. The pointed shadows of pines lay dark across the roadway, and sunlight, filtering through the trees, turned the carpet of russet needles to gold.

"Does she own the house?" Geneva inquired.

"She just takes care of it," Ginnie explained.

They turned into still another road. Ginnie saw the tawny elegance of tiger lilies by the wayside and a deep glade filled with wild pink roses. They passed an old white house set back from the road, and then Mrs. Evans signaled with her hand that she was about to turn into a driveway. The three cars pulled up before a snug little house of weathered gray shingles with gay red blinds. Mrs. Evans got out of her car and unlocked the door for them.

Ginnie, with Geneva close behind her, was first inside. They explored quickly. There was a roomy, comfortable living room with a fireplace; and a dining area at one end adjoined the little kitchen. There was one bedroom and a bath downstairs. Upstairs the girls found two more rooms.

"Look, Geneva, a double-decker!" Ginnie cried. "This is our room. Which do you want, upper or lower?"

Geneva picked the upper berth, and then Mrs. Porter called and they went flying downstairs to help unload the car.

"If you need anything," Mrs. Evans was saying at the door, "just let me know. My boy Ernie, he

cuts the grass and does any little repair jobs. You just let me know. Oh, you need an extra key."

Ginnie gazed in astonishment as Mrs. Evans extracted an enormous bunch of keys from her capacious old pocketbook.

"What a big bunch of keys!" she exclaimed.

Mrs. Evans laughed. "Have got quite a lot, haven't I?" she said. "I've got a few houses to look after." She removed a key from the big ring and handed it to Mrs. Fellows. "There." She paused on the step, shading her eyes with a worn brown hand, and looked across at the next yard. Ginnie could hear the whir of a lawn mower now. "There's Ernie," Mrs. Evans said, "cutting Miss Wade's grass."

"Who is our next-door neighbor?" Ginnie's mother asked, stepping outside too.

"Miss Wade. She's very nice. She's a teacher, or used to be. Always lived in that house, Miss Wade has. She likes youngsters." Mrs. Evans smiled at the two girls. "Used to be Ernie's Sunday-school teacher. Well, I'll step over and speak to my son for a minute. And if you need anything, don't forget, you call me. Miss Wade has a phone."

When she had gone they set about unloading. Ginnie toiled upstairs with her bag, while Geneva labored with coats and sweaters and the armful of books they had brought for rainy days. Daddy and Mr. Porter carried heavy suitcases to the bedrooms and deposited boxes of bedding. Mother and Mrs. Porter hung up clothes.

"Is that all?" Ginnie cried, running downstairs and outdoors. Both cars stood with doors and baggage compartments open.

"That's all," Daddy said. "And I don't know about the rest of you, but I'm hot! I'm ready for a swim!"

"Me too!" Ginnie cried. "Geneva!" she shouted at the foot of the stairs. "We're going swimming!"

Everyone was eager to go. There was no use in wasting a lovely afternoon, especially when Daddy and Mr. Porter had to go home tomorrow. They would be back week ends, and later for two whole weeks.

"We'll have to find out where the beach is," Mrs. Porter said.

Ginnie rushed upstairs to pull out a bathing suit. She could hardly wait to get to the beach. Already she could imagine the silky feel of the water lapping her body. A lovely breeze with a cool, dry edge, carrying the sweet smell of honeysuckle, blew the fish-net curtains, but it would be blazing hot on the sand.

"We have to find out where the beach is," she remarked to Geneva, who was already stepping into her suit. Ginnie quickly pulled on her own suit. "Now where's my cap? Oh, I don't need it!" She was too excited to take time looking for it. "I'm ready."

"So'm I. Where are the towels? Downstairs, I guess. Come on!" They were down before the grownups were ready.

"I know what," Ginnie said. "Let's go over and ask that boy Ernie where the beach is."

"O.K."

They crossed the grass, cool and prickly beneath their bare feet. A tall, lanky lad in faded blue jeans and a shirt wet with perspiration was pushing a lawn mower.

"Hi," Geneva said.

He looked up, startled, said "hi," and went on with his job.

"We came to ask you something," Ginnie said, keeping pace beside him. "We just got here. We live in that house next door. Would you mind telling us where the beach is, where we swim?"

Ernie had to stop then, although he did not look eager to talk. He's shy, Ginnie thought. He's about seventeen, and he's shy.

"You want the ocean or the bay?" he inquired.

"Which is which?" Geneva asked.

"Ocean's rough, and it's awful cold. Bay's smooth water and warmer."

"The bay," Ginnie said decidedly. She was not a strong swimmer, and she definitely did not like icy water.

"Pilgrim Cove's what you want then," Ernie said.

"Where is it?" Geneva asked.

"You go out to Route 6 and down a piece—maybe a mile and a half. You'll see a road to the left and a sign. Just keep to the left all the way and you'll come right there."

"Oh, thank you!" Ginnie said. " 'By now, see you later."

Their mothers and fathers had appeared, and

the girls dashed back. "I don't think he wants to see us later, though," Geneva giggled.

"Well, he looked very hot," Ginnie said. "He probably wishes he could go swimming instead of having to cut grass."

Ernie's directions took them to the bay in five minutes. The road ended in a sandy parking space, where a dozen cars stood gleaming in the sun. Beyond the path through the grass-grown dunes the bay lay sparkling. The girls ran ahead and stood gazing about with delight.

This was a narrow curve of white sand, sheltered by the rise of dunes behind it. Family groups dotted the beach, their gay umbrellas slanted against the sun. Small children dug their shovels in the smooth, wet sand at the water's edge. Heads bobbed in the dancing water.

Then the girls' parents were there, and Mr. Porter was screwing a big striped umbrella into the supporting sand. Mother and Mrs. Porter dropped gratefully into its shade.

But Ginnie and Geneva were on their way into the bay, running and laughing until the water creeping up to their waists slowed them down

and made them squeal at the cold. Then Ginnie boldly dropped on her knees and let the water rise quickly over her shoulders and chin. She struck out for deeper water, laughing at Geneva.

"Oh, Geneva!" she gasped. "It's heavenly!"

Their fathers were swimming farther out. After a while Ginnie waded out of the water and sat down breathless at the edge of the beach, letting the warm swells swing her about. She felt rested soon and stood up, surveying the curve of shore.

To her right, as she faced inland, the sand cliffs stretched into the distance. They were topped by a row of cottages with flights of wooden steps leading up to them, and the flights of steps grew longer as the cliffs rose higher.

To the left the bathing beach ended where a bar of sand and rocks extended into the water. Beyond that Ginnie could not see, for the shore curved. "Let's take a walk," she said, as Geneva came out of the water. "Let's explore around that point."

Off the jetty a huge rock, taller than the girls, was beginning to show in the water, for the tide was going out. They splashed through the sun-warmed shallows between rocks and sand, digging their toes into the pebbly silt to send up muddy clouds. Minnows and their swift shadows fled before them.

Beyond the sand bar the bottom proved to be stony, and the girls trudged out of the water to stroll along the wet, hard-packed sand. The beach was pebbly here, so there were no bathers. Ginnie stooped to pick up a scallop shell, bleached white, and carried it along, reluctant to toss away the graceful thing.

They walked on and on, happy and companionably silent, eyes searching the wet sand for its treasures. Honey sniffed busily at this world of exciting new smells.

After a long time Ginnie raised her eyes and stood still, gazing out over the bay. To her right the dunes stretched at right angles to the beach, their creamy slopes topped by a low growth. They curved to throw a protecting arm across the little harbor and finally became only a sand bar, like a faint streak of light along the horizon. Above the beach and the dunes there was a long stretch of pine woodland.

Ginnie became aware suddenly that they had

come beyond the sound of voices and the sight of humans. There was only the ceaseless shush-shush-shush of small waves splashing along the shore, the rough whisper of sand blowing against dry seaweed, and the restless wind, pressing, pressing against her eardrums.

We've been gone a long time, Ginnie thought. "Let's go back," she said, breaking the queer silence with the sound of her own voice.

Mother and Mrs. Porter were ready to leave. "We just got here!" Geneva protested.

"You have weeks ahead of you," her mother told her. "Right now we've got to get some food in the house, or we won't have any breakfast."

"Breakfast! How about dinner?" Geneva demanded. "I'm starved!"

"We're going out to dinner," her father informed her. With food to look forward to, the girls left the beach less reluctantly.

Back at the house they slipped quickly out of their wet suits and into fresh cotton dresses. "Geneva," Ginnie said, combing back her wet hair, "let's go over and get acquainted with that lady next door, Miss Wade."

When their parents set out to do the marketing, the girls walked over to the next house. The closely clipped green lawn gave the fragrance of freshly cut grass, and Ernie was nowhere in sight now. They were approaching a screened porch at the side of the house when a voice spoke. "How do you do!"

Miss Wade had risen from a rocking chair and was holding the screened door open for them. She was not young, but her figure was slim and erect and her tanned face only comfortably lined. Miss Wade's gray hair was brushed back in a plain un-curled bob, and she wore the kind of simple print dress Ginnie associated with teachers. Her eyes were brown. Kind eyes, Ginnie thought.

"I was hoping my new neighbors would come to call. Do sit down and tell me your names. I'm Allison Wade."

"I'm Ginnie Fellows," Ginnie said, seating her-self.

"And I'm Geneva Porter."

"Ginnie and Geneva. That's easy. I see you've already been swimming."

"Oh yes, it was wonderful," Ginnie said. "But

we had to come home too early. Because we had to get some food in the house."

"Only we're going out to dinner. Someplace," Geneva contributed. "I don't know where."

"I can suggest a place," Miss Wade said.

"Where?" Ginnie asked.

"We're having a supper at the church tonight. Ham and baked beans and pie. Does that sound good?"

Ginnie was just beginning to feel ravenous and it did sound good. "Oh, Geneva," she cried, "let's ask if we can go there!"

"O.K." But Geneva was peering rather impolitely into Miss Wade's kitchen. "This is a real old-fashioned house, isn't it?" she said. "Could we see the inside of it?"

Ginnie hoped Miss Wade would not be offended at having her house called old-fashioned. "I love old-fashioned houses," she said.

"Oh, so do I," Geneva put in quickly.

"Come on in." Miss Wade led the way. "If you love old-fashioned houses, you'll like this one, though it's not as old as some. I still use the wood stove, you see."

The big kitchen, with its ancient black range and old sink, was a pleasant place. Red geraniums bloomed, and a rocker was drawn close to the window looking into the garden.

"The stove's hot!" Geneva said.

"That's the only way I get hot water," Miss Wade explained. "I know what you'd like to see —my organ."

She led the way through the dining room to the parlor. Delighted, the girls took turns sitting down at the organ, but the wheezy old keys refused to respond until Miss Wade pulled the stops and pumped out a familiar hymn.

"Oh, Geneva, see the old doll!" Ginnie cried.

Miss Wade let them hold her. "She was mine when I was a little girl."

"Did you live in this house?" Ginnie inquired.
"Yes."

"May we go upstairs?" Geneva inquired.

They went up the steep stairs and looked at the old-fashioned bedrooms. In the upper hall Geneva gazed at the ceiling. "What's that thing?"

"It's a trap door. You put up a ladder and climb through to get to the attic."

"Oh, I wish we could do that!" Geneva exclaimed.

Miss Wade laughed. "You can't today. But I'll tell you what. Someday while you're here on the Cape it's going to rain. And then you come over, and I'll let you go up in the attic."

"Good! What's up there?" Ginnie asked.

"Lots of old things. You might find some clothes to dress up in."

Through the window Ginnie saw the car drive in next door. "They're back," she said. "Geneva, let's ask if we can go to the church supper!"

"I'll walk over with you," Miss Wade offered.

They were going out the door to the porch when Ginnie suddenly stopped and looked down. "Oh, what a pretty shell!"

A pale-pink spiral shell held the door propped open. "It's old," Miss Wade said, following her gaze. "You can buy conch shells in every gift shop on the Cape, all polished up, but this one is very old. It has a story, too." She stooped. "You can hear the roar of the sea in it, you know."

She held it to Ginnie's ear, and sure enough, pressing closer to the graceful curve, Ginnie imagined she could hear the toss of infinitely far-away waves.

When Geneva had listened to the sea, the three strolled across the lawn together and Ginnie and Geneva introduced their new friend to their parents.

"And please can we go to the supper at Miss Wade's church?" Geneva begged. "They're going to have ham and baked beans and pie and I'm hungry enough to eat a horse—and how soon can we go?"

They all laughed, and decided that the church supper would be exactly right.

"We should go now," Miss Wade said, glancing at her wrist watch. "The first sitting was at five-thirty, so they're almost ready for the six-thirty crowd. Suppose I get my car—I've got a couple of pies in it—and you can follow me."

"Oh, could Geneva and I go in your car?" Ginnie asked.

"Come along."

Late sunshine slanted, golden, across the green lawns. A thrush trilled from a treetop and a quail whistled, "Bob-White!" The breeze from the sea was almost cold now and carried the scent of pine. Ginnie felt full of salt water and fresh air and at peace with the world. She and Geneva sat in the front seat with Miss Wade as she turned her old green car into the road.

Fortunately Miss Wade was driving slowly. At the next crossroad she stepped sharply on the brake, quickly putting an arm in front of Ginnie and Geneva. Ginnie saw a very old-fashioned car, seeming to appear from nowhere, snort noisily across their path and disappear down the road.

"He almost hit us!" Geneva cried indignantly, after a startled moment.

Miss Wade, shifting gears, looked to the right and the left, then turned the corner. Glancing up, Ginnie saw that her face was set.

"That Ernie Evans!" Miss Wade said tersely. "He's a good boy and works hard, but he needs a paddling. Hasn't got one grain of sense when it comes to tearing round in that car!"

CHAPTER 2

The Diary

THE lighthearted skies that had smiled so warmly on Ginnie's first day on the Cape turned threatening Sunday night. Daddy and Mr. Porter left in the Porter car to drive home for the week. Waving them on their journey, Ginnie could see the wet gray fog standing, a silent menace, above the road. There was a moon, but thin veils of cloud rode swiftly over it.

Monday morning she awoke to the steady drumming of rain on the roof outside the bedroom window. The air felt damp and cold, and she turned on her side, pulling the warm wool blanket closer about her shoulders with a shiver of comfort. This was a morning to sleep late.

When she opened her eyes again, she smelled coffee and heard a murmur of voices below. Above her there was a thump and a creak.

"Look at that rain!" said Geneva's voice, hoarse with sleep.

"I don't want to look at it," Ginnie retorted gloomily.

Both girls lay in their warm beds for a few moments, too drowsy and disgusted to talk. Then suddenly Ginnie flopped on her back, wide-awake. "Geneva! I just thought of something!"

"What?" said Geneva crossly.

"Miss Wade said we could go up in her attic when it rained!"

Geneva's reaction was prompt. "O.K.! Let's get up and go over there!"

They put on their shorts and sneakers and were downstairs in five minutes. Mother and Mrs. Porter were lingering over coffee. The lamps were lighted, and the comfortable living room seemed a bright and pleasant place this gloomy day.

Mother brought orange juice and cereal to the girls as they pulled chairs to the table, and Mrs. Porter slipped two slices of bread into the toaster.

"No swimming today, my friends," Mrs. Porter said.

"We don't care," said Geneva. "We've got plans."

"Oh?" her mother said.

"At least we think we have," Ginnie added. "If Miss Wade will let us. She said she would. We're going up in her attic."

"Now don't you bother Miss Wade," Mother protested. "You make sure you're not inconveniencing her."

They promised. Breakfast finished, they donned slickers and set out. It was still raining hard. From the chimney of the white house next door a thin feather of smoke spiraled, and a whiff of wood smoke hung cozily in the sodden air.

Miss Wade was washing her breakfast dishes. The kitchen, as they stamped in through the screened porch, felt delightfully warm. The old range gave off a mild, companionable crackle and seemed almost alive. "Oh, it feels good here!" Ginnie said.

"What are you young ones up to this morning?" Miss Wade asked, hanging her dish towel on the rack above the stove to dry. "What a shame you've got such a bad day!"

"Oh, we don't mind," Geneva assured her. "Do we, Ginnie? That is, we don't mind *if. . . .*"

"*If. . . .*" Ginnie continued. "Remember what you said we could do when it rained?"

"Oh!" Miss Wade threw back her head and laughed. "I can't get away with a thing, can I? Well, I don't know why you can't go up to the attic. Matter of fact, I was going up there anyway to see if the roof's leaking."

"Oh, good!" Geneva did a little jig of joy.

"Take off your raincoats," Miss Wade said. "I'm going to put on my old slacks for this excursion."

Shortly she led the way upstairs. The ladder had to be set up beneath the door in the ceiling and made secure. Then Miss Wade mounted. She pushed up the trap door and climbed through. "Just a minute," her voice said. They heard her move across the attic floor. "It's leaking. I'll have to get a pail." She came back to the attic entrance and backed down. "Go on up now if you want to. Careful."

Ginnie went first, with Geneva close behind her. As she climbed onto the attic floor, the rain pounding on the slanting roof seemed frighteningly close. Ginnie stood up and looked around.

There were two small windows through which the twilight of the gloomy morning filtered. In the dimness Ginnie could see a piece or two of broken furniture, three or four trunks, and some boxes.

"I've got to get a pail to catch this drip," Miss Wade repeated, mounting the ladder to look through the opening. "Now, you two, don't go into that trunk, please. Those are old family things I'm keeping. But here"—she indicated another trunk—"in this one are some clothes you may dress up in if you want to."

Ginnie raised the lid. The refreshing smell of moth balls rose from the contents, and she took a deep sniff.

"I don't think there's much else to interest you," Miss Wade said. "There are some old books in that box."

She left them then, and the two girls bent excitedly over the open trunk. They were already

pulling dresses over their heads when Miss Wade returned and handed up a pail to be set under the leak in the roof. She left them again, chuckling.

Fifteen minutes later, holding up long skirts and carrying dress-up shoes, Ginnie and Geneva cautiously descended the ladder. They paused to change their sneakers for the shoes, then felt their way down to the first floor and presented themselves to Miss Wade. She was making a pie.

"Mercy me! Did I ever wear anything that looked like that?"

They burst into gales of laughter. Ginnie straightened the large flat straw hat on her head and swished the dragging skirt that sagged about her ankles. Geneva pranced up and down in high-laced black shoes and a narrow dress whose hem line was down to the floor.

"Come on, Ginnie, let's find some more things," Geneva said.

They donned other dresses and hats and descended again to share their mirth with their new friend. The steady pounding of rain went on. Ginnie was putting one of the dresses back in the trunk when a large drop landed on top of her head.

She looked up at the rafters and another drop plopped onto her face.

"We'd better tell Miss Wade there's a new leak," she said.

"Wait till we go downstairs again," Geneva said. "I don't want to dress up any more right now. I'm going to look at these books."

She dragged the carton under the window and took off the dusty, yellowed newspaper that covered the books. Geneva picked up a slim leather-bound volume. "This just has old writing in it." She put it back and took out another book.

Idly Ginnie picked up the book Geneva had discarded. The pages, as she turned them, were yellowed with age, yet the writing stood out clearly. But it was such old-fashioned writing she could hardly read it. She was about to close the volume when a legible sentence leaped out at her, and she paused.

Uncle Frank, she read in the slanting, shaded hand, *will be home any day now. I can hardly wait to see the present he said he would bring me.* Ginnie went on reading in the dim light from the window, a slight wrinkle of concentration lining her forehead.

"These are stupid old books," Geneva was saying. "Come on, let's go down and do something else. Come on, Ginnie!" she repeated, as Ginnie seemed not to hear.

"What?" Ginnie was still reading. "Geneva," she said, her eyes on the book, "know what? This is somebody's diary. I think it was some girl's diary. And look how old it is!"

Geneva peered over her shoulder. "I can't read it. Anything interesting?"

"I don't know. It is very hard to make out."

"Bring it downstairs," Geneva said. "We can ask Miss Wade whose it was."

Miss Wade seemed dismayed at the news that another leak had developed. "Oh, dear," she said.

"You'll have to get a new roof," Geneva remarked cheerfully.

Their hostess glanced at her. "I'm afraid I shall," she said, but she did not sound happy.

I wonder if Miss Wade is poor, thought Ginnie. She looked around the shabby, spotless old room from this new viewpoint. The kitchen was filled with a fruity fragrance. Miss Wade opened the oven door, and the good smell of browning pie crust drifted out.

They showed her the book. She took it in her hands. "Oh! Do you know what this is? It's my mother's diary, when she was a little girl. I'd forgotten it was up there." She turned to the inside of the front cover. "Look at the date—1871. She was ten years old when she kept this diary."

"Not even as old as we are," Geneva commented. "But I can't read that old-fashioned writing."

"I can," Ginnie said. "If you go slow it's not too hard. Please can I see it again, Miss Wade?"

"Go and sit on the sofa in the dining room," their hostess told them. "Turn on the lamp. I'm going up to put something under that miserable leak."

But Geneva was not interested in the diary. She picked up a magazine from the table and Ginnie sat alone, puzzling over the old, slanted writing. It was such elegant, careful writing for a little girl. She read on, slowly making out the words.

Suddenly Ginnie spoke. "Geneva, listen to this!"

"H'm?" Geneva was absorbed in a story.

"Are you listening?"

"Yes, go ahead."

"Listen to what this says. *My dolly, that Uncle Frank brought me from Paris, has a precious jewel.*" Ginnie paused.

"Well, go on!"

"*But,*" Ginnie went on reading, "*sh! It's a secret!*"

"Go on!" Geneva said impatiently.

"That's all she says about it. The next part is about something else."

The girls gazed at one another. "Do you suppose her doll really did have a precious jewel?" Ginnie said.

"Let's ask Miss Wade." They could hear her coming downstairs.

Suddenly Ginnie sat up straight. "Maybe that doll in the parlor is the one in the diary."

Miss Wade appeared. "Miss Wade," Geneva burst out, as they followed her into the kitchen, "in your mother's old diary she says something about a doll that her Uncle Frank brought her from Paris. Is that the doll in the parlor that you showed us?"

Miss Wade was taking her pie from the oven now. She set it on the table and stood looking at the girls for a moment before she spoke.

"No," she said then, and Ginnie thought there was a strange note in her voice. "The one in the parlor was my own doll." She laid her pot holder down. "But I used to have that doll of my mother's." And then Miss Wade sat down at the table, folded her hands, and gazed into space as if she were seeing the doll.

"Her name was Lady Vanderbilt. She was a beautiful big lady doll, and she wore a sweeping lavender taffeta gown with a train caught up with a tiny bunch of flowers, and a lace fichu at the neck."

"Oh!" Ginnie breathed.

"Did she really come from Paris?" Geneva asked.

"Yes. Uncle Frank was a sea captain. He sailed everywhere—the South Seas, Europe, the West Indies—and he brought my mother presents from everywhere. He was a queer duck, I guess, but he was very fond of my mother."

"I wish you still had that doll," Ginnie said.

"Where is she?" Geneva demanded.

Miss Wade glanced down at her hands, and for a moment Ginnie thought that she was not going to answer. "She disappeared," she said finally. "Years ago—oh, thirty years ago—I went to Europe one summer and I let this house to some people from California. Lady Vanderbilt was put away in a trunk up in the attic. Sarah Brooks—she worked for me then; she was Ernie's grandmother —Sarah had wrapped her up carefully and put her away. When I looked for her months later she was gone."

"Didn't you try to get her back?" Ginnie asked in dismay.

"Well, so much time had passed by then. The Lamberts—the people who had the house—had gone back to California. There were a couple of children in the family and I thought—well, perhaps they got hold of the doll and broke her. Or maybe they took her with them. I hated to make a fuss. And my mother was gone by then. So. . . ." Miss Wade raised her hands in a little futile gesture. "I just forgot about Lady V."

There was a pause. Ginnie gave a deep sigh. "She must have been just beautiful."

For the moment, thinking about the lovely Lady V, they had forgotten the jewel mentioned in the diary. Now Ginnie remembered it, and at the same moment Geneva said, "In the diary it says. . . ."

But suddenly, behind Miss Wade's back, Ginnie was shaking her head violently at Geneva, a finger on her lips. Why, she hardly knew, except that she did not want to discuss the jewel right now with Miss Wade. There was a slight sense of mystery about that note in the diary. Deep in her heart Ginnie did not want that mystery immediately dispelled by some simple explanation.

Geneva looked startled, but she obeyed the signal, finishing somewhat lamely. "It says—oh, I forget."

Suddenly Ginnie wanted to talk to Geneva alone. "We'd better go home," she said. "We've had a lovely time, Miss Wade. May I leave the diary down here and read some more in it some other time?"

Miss Wade nodded. "You may, my dear. I'll put it on the table in the parlor." She got up to carry her pie into the pantry, and Ginnie leaned forward to sniff the warm aroma of fruit rising from it.

"Did those blueberries grow around here?" Geneva asked, peering into a bowl of berries on the table.

"No, but Cape blueberries will be along in August. A few of the beach plums are getting ripe now. They're early this year."

"What are beach plums?" Geneva wanted to know.

"I'll show you when they get ripe. They grow everywhere on the Cape and they make wonderful jelly. Don't you know Cape Cod is famous for beach-plum jelly?"

"Sounds delicious," Ginnie said. "I wish we could pick some and make some jelly."

"Why don't you?" Miss Wade asked.

"Don't know how."

"Well now, I'll tell you." Miss Wade stepped to a cupboard and took down a glass of deep crimson jelly. "You take this home and eat it with your breakfast. If you like it, we'll go out and pick beach plums someday and I'll help you make jelly. I'll be making some, anyway."

"But look at all you've got!" Ginnie cried, gazing in amazement at the cupboard shelves. "Why do you want to make any more?"

Miss Wade laughed. "Well, you see," she said, "beach-plum jelly is a little project of mine. I make it, and I sell it to whoever wants to buy it, and then I give the money to the church."

"All the money?" Geneva asked.

"Most of it."

Miss Wade is nice, Ginnie thought, a warm feeling of affection coming over her. She's got leaks in her roof, so she can't have much money, but she gives the jelly money to the church instead of keeping it.

"I'd adore to pick beach plums," she said. "Come on, Geneva, we've just got to go home and have lunch."

"Come again, children," Miss Wade said.

Ginnie paused at the door for a moment to lift the conch shell and hold it to her ear. "I love that!" she remarked, putting it down. "Well, thank you for everything, Miss Wade."

"We had a wonderful time," Geneva added.

Rain was still falling, but the downpour had slackened. They held their slickers over their heads, not bothering to put them on.

"Geneva," Ginnie said in a cautious voice, as they walked slowly along, splashing through every puddle in their boots, "I'll bet that doll really did have a precious jewel. Because somebody stole her out of the attic, and I'll bet they stole her to get the jewel!"

Geneva looked around from under her slicker in astonishment. "Ginnie! Why, Miss Wade's mother wrote that diary ten million years ago, ages before the doll was lost!"

Ginnie hesitated. She really was a little confused. But Geneva was right. The diary had been written when Miss Wade's mother was a girl ten years old. The doll had disappeared after her mother had died, an old lady. Of course there was no connection. She was disappointed.

"You're right." She was thoughtful a moment. "Do you think there really was a precious jewel?"

"How should I know?" They reached the house and Geneva pulled open the screen door.

If there had been one, many, many years ago, whatever became of it, Ginnie wondered? Perhaps Miss Wade still had it. But somehow Miss Wade did not seem like a person who owned a precious jewel. Her roof leaked. . . . If there really had been a jewel, probably she, or her mother, had sold it and spent the money long ago. Yes, of course they had.

She stepped into the house. And suddenly the words in that old careful yet childish writing flashed before her eyes once more with an odd persistence.

Sh! It's a secret!

CHAPTER 3

Beach Plums and Quahogs

THE rain blew out to sea during the night, and the days that followed were filled with dazzling sun, cloudless skies, and winds that whitecapped the bay.

Ginnie thought of the days as having different colors. There were the blue-and-gold mornings at Pilgrim Cove, when the bowl of the sky was a burning sapphire and all the ripples and small breaking waves far out on the bay's surface flashed like cut crystal.

There were the gray-and-purple days, when the bay lay dark and sullen under cloudy skies and the water felt delightfully warm when you worked up courage to go in.

And there was a rough, exciting kind of day that Ginnie exulted in, when she went down to the beach to look but not to swim. She hugged a coat about her, and could hardly tell whether the white ruffles on the pewter surface of the bay were white-caps or gulls, because both were out there riding the wind-rocked waters. When the tide was 'way out, there were hundreds of gulls feasting on spider crabs, fighting each other, stealing and chasing. The wild wind was strong with the smell of the shellfish and loud with the raucous cries of the birds.

Their days were governed by the tide table. It was on a morning when the tide was too low for swimming at Pilgrim Cove that Miss Wade appeared, broad sun hat on her head, a basket on her arm. The two girls and their mothers, lazing in the sunshine at the back of the house, got up as their neighbor approached.

"Sit down, sit down!" Miss Wade waved them down but sat on the edge of the chair Ginnie provided. "I just wondered whether anyone was interested in picking beach plums this morning. There are a few ripe now."

"Yes!" Geneva cried.

"Me too!" Ginnie echoed.

"I'm afraid I'm too lazy," Mother said.

Mrs. Porter smiled at them. "We'll let you girls do the work."

"Better put on your jeans," Miss Wade advised. "You'll get your legs scratched in the bushes. I have some buckets you can take."

The three set out in Miss Wade's car and drove through the shade of the woods to a sunny road not far from the bay. They could see the water across the low marshes, a crinkled silver blue under the sun, stretching far out into the morning mist.

Miss Wade brought the car to a stop. "We'll find enough here to keep us busy for a while," she said.

The loaded bushes ran along the road for a hundred yards and as far back as Ginnie could see. Miss Wade showed her how to strip the hard, rosy fruit from the stem. "These are just nice," she said. "They won't jell if they're too ripe."

It was hot work, but such fun to wander deeper and deeper into the bushes, seeing the pails fill. The little plums were so pretty, with their rich color ranging from green and blue to deepest crimson and purple, that Ginnie kept holding up twigs to show Geneva and Miss Wade. "I'm going to take these home and put them in water for a bouquet," she said, breaking off more branches and admiring the lovely blush of the plums.

When they had enough, Ginnie was glad to get into the car again. Her arms were stung by the scratchy bushes, she was sunburned, and it felt good to get out of the hot sun and sit down. She brushed the perspiration from her face and turned to look with satisfaction at the full buckets of beach plums.

"We can make loads of jelly, can't we?" she said happily.

"We haven't got any jelly glasses," Geneva remarked.

"I've got hundreds," Miss Wade assured them. "Everyone gives me jelly glasses."

"But we won't make jelly today," Ginnie said. "I can't wait to get to the beach, I'm so hot!"

"They'll keep," Miss Wade said. "Anyhow, you've done one of the things everybody does on the Cape. You've picked beach plums."

Ginnie considered that. "What are the other things everybody does on the Cape? Besides swimming, of course."

"Oh, clamming, I suppose."

Geneva sat up straight. "Let's go clamming!"

"Could we?" Ginnie looked up.

"You certainly can if you want to. You have to get permits and you can rent rakes."

"Where would we go clamming?" Geneva inquired.

"On almost any beach."

"Oh, will you come with us?" Ginnie cried.

Miss Wade laughed. "I haven't been clamming for years. You children are going to bring back my lost youth. Yes, I'll go clamming if you want to. We'll have to ask your mothers to stop in at the town hall and get permits."

"Oh, Miss Wade, I just love you!" Ginnie cried, snuggling closer to her new friend's shoulder.

"Thank you very much." Miss Wade gave her a sideways smile as she turned into the driveway.

Next morning, when the two girls and their mothers drove into town to do the marketing, Ginnie thought of the permits.

"All right," Mother said. "Let's all get permits and go clamming."

"And get one for Miss Wade, too," Ginnie said, "because she's just going on our account."

They came out of the white town hall with their permits and strolled along the busy village street toward the parking lot. They walked past the grocery and fruit store, its sidewalk crowded with crates of lettuce and peaches, past the little blue-painted restaurant, the gift shop, the dry-goods store. They paused at the town bulletin board and read the notices of church suppers, baby sitters, boats for rent.

"Look, Mother," Ginnie said, reading aloud. *"Auction of antiques and things.* And 'things,' that's funny! Can we go? I've never been to an auction."

"Why not?" Mother said.

Just beyond the bulletin board was the old house where the Historical Society had its museum. Mother paused. "This is open today. Let's see what's in here."

They opened the screen door to a quiet room, and the musty smell of great age rose to greet them.

An elderly gentleman at the desk looked up over his spectacles. Then he drew them off and got up. "Good morning," he said.

He was delighted to show them around. There were spinning wheels and old wooden churns from Cape houses and a cobbler's bench with its tools. There were models of sailing ships, nautical instruments, and ships' lanterns. The glass cases around the walls held Sandwich glass and old, beautiful copper lusterware.

Wandering along, Ginnie stopped to read a framed document hanging on the wall. It was a copy of the Pilgrim Compact. *Haveing undertaken for ye glorie of God, and advancement of ye Christian faith, and honor of our King and Countrie. . . .* With a little thrill of recognition she read the signatures—Miles Standish, John Alden. . . .

"Look, Ginnie," Geneva was saying, peering into one of the cases. "Here's a diary like Miss Wade's mother's."

The curator heard her, and he looked interested. "Are you people friends of Miss Wade?"

"We're next-door summer neighbors," Mother explained. "She's been lovely to the girls."

The old gentleman nodded. "Fine person. Wonderful woman. Old Cape Cod family, of course, fine family. Impoverished now."

Ginnie felt a shock. *Impoverished*—what a terrible word! Miss Wade impoverished! She and Geneva had seen that their friend did not have much money. But *impoverished* gave her a dreadful feeling somewhere in her stomach.

"I don't suppose," Mrs. Porter was saying thoughtfully, "there are many ways for people like Miss Wade to earn a living here."

"No. Summer roomers, of course. Doing things for the summer people."

"Like Mrs. Evans does," Geneva said.

The old gentleman nodded at her. "Mrs. Evans, yes," he said. "Widowed young. Had a hard time bringing up that boy of hers. Eat up in the winter what they earn in the summer. See Ernie tearing around here, burning up gasoline, but you can't stop these young people when they get car crazy. He's a good boy, though," he added. "Wants to go to college, but I doubt if he'll make it."

"Are you a native of the Cape?" Mother asked, interested.

The old gentleman shook his head. "I've summered here for forty years though. Now I live here the year round. Emerson's my name, Dr. Emerson. Used to spend my time on the beach, picking up specimens of sea life. Biology and zoology are my field—taught for years. Now I'm quite content to look after this little museum. Passes the time very nicely. Would you like to go upstairs?"

Upstairs the girls found patchwork quilts, old jewelry, and exquisite hand-embroidered nightcaps of sheerest lawn.

"Look!" Ginnie exclaimed, gazing at a display of old United States money. "Did you know there used to be ten-cent *bills?*" She and Geneva giggled delightedly over this discovery.

The skeleton of an Indian lay in a glass case. His bones, the girls learned, had been found under layers of sand and shale. They stood gazing down. "How do they know he was an Indian?" Geneva commented. "Looks like just anybody."

They bade Dr. Emerson good morning. "Come in any time," he urged cordially. "Delighted to have you."

"He's nice," Geneva said as they went down the walk. "Everybody's nice up here."

"Which beach are we going to today?" Mother asked, as they got into the car.

"Pilgrim Cove," Ginnie said instantly.

"Yes," Geneva agreed.

They had visited every beach in the vicinity. On weekends, when their fathers were there, they sometimes turned toward the sea. Here the broad beach lay far below the steep bluff and the girls raced down through the loose, hot sand while the grownups toiled through the dunes lugging lunch and the beach umbrella. Even at low tide the waves were too mountainous, the shelving shore too steep, for Ginnie to swim, though she loved the thunderous excitement of the rearing, crashing breakers.

But Ginnie loved Pilgrim Cove best. She was constantly enchanted by the endless procession of events there. If they went down early in the morning and the tide was right, the clammers were out with rakes and pails. Then, with the incoming tide, came the mothers and toddling sun-browned babies clutching pails, small boys with nets to capture crabs, and bigger boys and girls with skin-diver masks and snorkels. There were rowboats coming and going, and speedboats zoomed to and fro towing water skiers. Ginnie always watched anxiously until the skiers landed safely in the shallows and dropped their lines.

There was the excitement and mystery of watching the tide come in. Ginnie loved to sit calmly while the water crept higher and higher—not steadily, but in sudden angry little spurts—knowing that at one magic moment—the tide table told when—the water would suddenly stop rising and gradually begin to slide back into the depths. She never got over the wonder.

Today, as she and Geneva sat on the sand, they watched two young people, a man and a girl, put a kayak together. The two paddled off in the low, fragile-looking craft, and the young man called, "O.K., Portugal, here we come!"

This afternoon they lingered late. The sun-browned babies and their mothers went away and the beach lay deserted. But the day's drama was not over, for two fishermen brought in their stripers, pulled their boat out of the water, and carried the outboard motor away.

"It's getting chilly. Come on, children," Mother said finally, beginning to gather towels. Mrs. Porter got to her feet and collapsed the beach umbrella.

Ginnie gave a sad little sigh. This was the best, the most beautiful part of the day. The air felt cool when she sat up, but the sand still held the day's warmth and the wind had dropped. A path of molten gold led straight across the silken water to the setting sun.

Miss Wade said they must go clamming when the tide was 'way out, so they set forth early one morning, taking their lunch along. They wore their bathing suits. "I'm taking you to a place where we'll have to wade out to the flats," Miss Wade explained, "and the water will be fairly deep when we come back."

They carried pails to put the clams in, and stopped at the hardware store to rent their rakes. Mother was driving, and Miss Wade guided her past the town beach, along roads and through beach colonies they had not seen before. This, Ginnie realized, gazing out at the water, was the arm of dune land she saw from the beach. The long graceful hook of sand curved far out into the bay. The dunes rose high above the water and the green bluffs were dotted with attractive summer homes.

"This is Tecumseh Neck," Miss Wade told them. "Lovely place to see the sunset, out at the tip. Now let's park right here."

"There's someone clamming," Geneva cried.

"We're ahead of the crowd, though," Miss Wade said.

They left the lunch on the beach. "We can eat here when we get through," Miss Wade said. "All right, got your pails and rakes? Better keep your sneakers on," she advised, as Geneva moved to take hers off. You're going out where it's mucky."

"Come on!" Ginnie could not wait to begin. "Where shall we start?"

"Let's try right over here in the wet sand and see what we get before we go out farther." Miss Wade shaded her eyes with a hand. "The flats are still under water, anyway."

They trailed down the beach and Miss Wade showed them how to use the rake. "Don't dig deep. See, you just rake the surface lightly, and sooner or later you'll strike something that feels like a stone, and—there's something!"

She stooped, felt in the wet sand, and pried up a sand-encrusted object. Brushing the sand off, she showed it to them. "There you are! A good big quahog."

"I'm going to try," Ginnie announced. "I'm going over here. You go the other way, Geneva."

The group spread out. Excited, Ginnie set her pail down and took up the rake, gently scraping the sand surface as Miss Wade had showed them. It was wet here near the edge of the beach, and water quickly seeped up to fill the tracks of the rake. Ginnie drew the prongs over the sand, moving down the beach as she did so.

There was a shout from Geneva. "I've got one! Look, Mother! Look, Ginnie!"

Ginnie glanced up, then went back to raking, spurred to new vigor. She raked and raked, but plowed up nothing but sand. Finally she stopped, discouraged. "I can't find a single clam!" she cried.

Miss Wade came over. "Are you working too hard at it? Look for little holes in the sand. And do it gently, like this. Suppose we try farther out."

Ankle-deep in the clear, sun-warmed water, they raked away, bringing up clouds of mud. Suddenly Ginnie's rake struck stone. "Oh, I've got something!" she gasped.

It was a clam, but too small, Miss Wade said reluctantly, to keep. "They have to be—oh, so big—or it's against the law to keep them. But you'll get some. Just keep at it."

"I'm going over *there!*" Ginnie said firmly.

"Perhaps you're moving too far away," Miss Wade suggested. "The others seem to be finding clams."

But Ginnie stubbornly picked her own patch of sand. She was completely discouraged by the time Miss Wade said they could wade out to the flats.

"Look, I've got ten clams!" Geneva showed Ginnie her pail.

"How are you doing, dear?" Mother inquired. "Look at all I've got."

"Well, I haven't got one," Ginnie said, humiliated. But she waded through the water with the

others, deeper and deeper, dragging her empty pail. The water rose to her waist and higher. Then it grew shallower again and finally they all waded out onto the wet island. Again they spread out and went to work. Miss Wade stayed with Ginnie.

Ginnie dug up oysters. But Miss Wade said they were much too small to eat this time of year. At last Ginnie straightened with a tired sigh. She wasn't going to find any clams; that was clear.

A man came wading toward the flats. He did not pause where Ginnie was but tramped straight across the little island to the far side. Resting, Ginnie saw him begin to rake and almost immediately stoop to toss a clam into his bucket.

"I'm going over there," she announced to Miss Wade.

She had scarcely drawn her rake across the coarse sand when she hit what felt like a rock. Excited, Ginnie dropped her rake and groped through the sand with her fingers. It took both hands to pry it up, and it was a quahog, a big one. "Oh, boy!" Ginnie said out loud, thrilled.

From then on her luck changed. Each stroke of

the rake discovered clams. Ginnie worked steadily, her heart beating happily now. She was so far
from the others that nobody knew how well she
was doing.

It's just like digging for buried treasure, she
thought, spirits soaring as she pried up another
shell with grimy hands.

She worked on and on, her pail filling, until she
saw Miss Wade coming toward her. "We'll have
to start back," Miss Wade called. "The tide's coming in. How are you doing?"

Ginnie waited, beaming, for her to come up.
"Why, your pail is full!" Miss Wade exclaimed.

They had all done well, but Ginnie had the
most. Her pail was so heavy that she could hardly
carry it. Carry it she did, however, with both
hands, as she waded into the water and headed for
shore. Then the water grew deeper and she could
not lift the pail high enough. She was afraid the
clams would float out and away, so Mother and
Miss Wade took the bucket, carrying it between
them.

The water was much deeper than when they had
waded out. Ginnie, trailing her mother and Miss

Wade, had a frightening moment when the water came over her shoulders. She stood still, panic-stricken, until she saw that Geneva, up front, was well out of the water now. She took a tentative step forward and the water receded. Then she was wading out onto the beach to join the others.

"Ginnie, isn't it fun!" Geneva shouted. "We can have gallons of clam chowder!"

"Oh, it was wonderful!" Ginnie said. "Oh, I just *love* clamming! I want to come every day!"

CHAPTER 4

The Auction

GINNIE strolled outdoors into the fresh morning, nibbling buttered toast and beach-plum jelly, and stood looking at the day.

Under her bare feet the grass lay drenched from the night mists, but overhead the clouds were hastily crowding to the horizon, preparing the blue sky for a perfect day. The quail were calling. "Bob-White! Bob-White!"

This was the day of the auction—the sale of "antiques and things" at the church. Ginnie saw Miss Wade cross her yard, pruning shears in hand, and went over to say good morning.

"We're going to the auction today," she said.

"Better go early," Miss Wade advised. "Anything good is always snapped up."

"Aren't you going?"

"No, I'm not."

"Why?"

"I never go to auctions." Miss Wade's shears were cutting roses. "Take these to your mother."

Ginnie accepted the two pink roses and drew in a deep breath of their sharply sweet old-fashioned fragrance. She wiped a drop of dew from her nose. "Why don't you ever go to auctions, Miss Wade?"

"Auctions are bad for people who haven't any money to spend."

"We have some money to spend, Geneva and I," Ginnie told her. "We counted it, and we've got five dollars between us!"

"Won't you have fun getting rid of that!" Miss Wade straightened and started toward the house, her hands full of the dew-sprinkled roses. "Have a lovely day, dear."

"We'll come and show you what we buy," Ginnie called, turning and skipping home.

She reported Miss Wade's advice to go early. "I have to get to the bank this morning," Mother said.

"Why don't we drop the girls at the auction?"

Mrs. Porter suggested. "They can save us some seats and we'll get back as soon as we can."

Early as it was, they found the church parking lot already filled with cars, and the lawn crowded with people milling about and examining the sale objects which were laid out on tables. There were older women in light summer dresses and younger ones whose brown legs looked long and slim in shorts. The men seemed very happy and carefree, Ginnie thought, in their shorts or slacks and gay sport shirts.

"Have fun," Mother said, as she and Mrs. Porter dropped the girls at the church parking lot. "We'll be back shortly."

As they headed for the display of articles to be sold, Ginnie paused for a moment. "Isn't that a cute car!" She was looking at a low red sports model.

Geneva nodded. "It's a Jaguar," she said, reading the name.

They went up on the church lawn and stood looking around, a bit uncertainly. "Where shall we look first?" Ginnie wondered. A woman, hurrying past with a pile of paper-wrapped sandwiches, paused. "There's a table of clothes and things over there you might like to see, girls," she said, nodding toward a booth at the far side of the lawn. "And that table has books. Lots of good bargains, and you can buy them right now." Then she indicated another counter. "Those things are going to be auctioned later, you know, so see if there's anything you want to bid on."

"Oh, thank you," Ginnie said. "Let's look at the clothes, Geneva."

Ginnie found a pair of red-and-white striped seersucker shorts. When she held them up they seemed exactly her size. She looked at the price tag. "Fifty cents! I'm going to buy these."

Geneva bought two old books for ten cents apiece.

"These must be 'things,' " Ginnie said, giggling. "I like things better than antiques, but my mother likes antiques."

"So does mine," said Geneva. "Come on, let's look at them. I might find something for Mother's birthday."

The objects to be auctioned were displayed on a long counter. There were brass andirons, old chairs rather the worse for wear, glass and china and old tarnished silver. The girls pushed along, uninterested.

They came to a doll's cradle. "Oh, cute!" Geneva said, and set it gently rocking. "Wouldn't you like to have this, Ginnie?"

"Uh-huh," Ginnie said agreeably. Farther along she saw some dolls, and she went on to examine them. She picked up a baby doll in long clothes, cuddled it lovingly, and laid it down. She put out her hand for a rag doll. Then, suddenly, Ginnie stood perfectly still.

"Geneva!" she said after a moment.

"What?"

"Look!"

She was staring at a doll. It was a large old-fashioned doll, and clearly it was not a thing, but an antique. The doll wore a faded lavender gown of taffeta, long and sweeping. There was a lace fichu at her neck. And the skirt was caught up with a tiny bunch of yellowed flowers.

For a long moment both girls gazed at the doll. "It's Miss Wade's mother's doll," Geneva said in a whisper.

"It must be," said Ginnie. "Lady Vanderbilt! She's just the way Miss Wade said!" She touched the doll gently, too awed to pick her up.

"Oh-h!" Geneva looked around anxiously, seeking advice. "What are we going to do? We've got to buy her!"

They had not noticed that people were fast filling the seats facing the auctioneer's stand until the sound of a man's voice announced that the auction was about to begin.

"Oh, it's beginning," Ginnie said. "Geneva, when they auction this doll, we've *got* to buy her! Oh, I wish Mother would hurry! Come on, let's sit down."

They saved two seats, but there was no sign of their mothers. The auction began. Ginnie had never attended an auction before, and she watched and listened, fascinated, as the auctioneer maneuvered the bids higher and higher. She even forgot momentarily about the doll, it was all so exciting. Now he was auctioning the andirons.

"Here's a fine old set of brass andirons. Beautiful for any home, anywhere. Only need a little

cleaning up. Really fine set. Who'll give me ten dollars for these beautiful andirons?"

"Two dollars," a voice said without great interest.

"Two dollars, that starts it. Who'll give me three?"

"Two fifty."

"Three!"

Voices were speaking up now from different parts of the audience. "Three fifty!"

"I'm offered three dollars and fifty cents for these antique brass andirons worth many times the price. Who'll give me four dollars? Four dollars over here! Who'll give me five? Five fifty?"

The andirons were sold for six dollars, and Ginnie breathed a sigh of relief as the suspense ended. She watched anxiously for the next object to be auctioned.

The auctioneer did a clever job of spacing out the real buys. In between the good brass and glass and furniture came cheap household items, an electric toaster needing repair, cracked china, and ugly Victorian oak furniture.

Ginnie kept looking anxiously around for her

mother and Mrs. Porter. "I wish they'd come before he gets to the doll!" she said to Geneva.

Suddenly Geneva clutched her arm. "There's the doll! That man just handed it to him. Oh, I can't stand it, I'm so excited! I'm going to bid!"

"We can only bid up to five dollars, Geneva, that's all, don't forget. Oh, where are they?" Ginnie moaned, standing up and searching the crowd for her mother.

The auctioneer was holding up the doll. "Here is a really lovely thing. A beautiful old doll that dates back a long, long time. Probably a hundred years old." He fingered the doll's gown. "Clothes still in good condition. Doll's been well taken care of. Somebody loved her. Here's a real treasure. Who'll start the bidding on this beautiful doll?"

Ginnie's voice suddenly choked in her throat. There was no response for a minute. Then she heard from beside her, "One dollar!" and knew that Geneva was bidding.

"One dollar. The little girl bids a dollar to start it. Who'll raise that?"

And then, far back in the crowd, a woman's voice spoke. "Two dollars."

Ginnie's heart leaped into her throat and thumped wildly. "Three dollars!" she shouted, finding her voice.

"Three dollars." The auctioneer held the doll high. "Who'll give me. . . ."

"Three and a quarter," the voice from the back called.

"Three fifty!" Geneva yelled.

"Three fifty. Who'll bid four dollars?"

The voice in the crowd responded. "Three seventy-five." Ginnie moaned.

Geneva was not giving up. "Four."

"Four and a quarter."

"Four fifty!" Geneva shouted and suddenly clapped a hand to her mouth.

From the rear came, "Four seventy-five."

Ginnie drew a deep breath. Her hands clutched the back of the chair in front of her. "Five dollars!" she heard herself cry shrilly.

"Five dollars. This beautiful old doll is a give-away at five dollars. Who'll give me more?"

"Ginnie!" Geneva gripped her arm and whispered hoarsely. "We haven't got five dollars! Don't you remember we spent seventy cents?"

"Going at five dollars," intoned the auctioneer. "Going at five dollars. Going. . . ."

"Six dollars!" The bidder in the rear was not giving up either.

"Six. Anyone give me more?" The gavel hovered in the air as the auctioneer waited a brief second, then banged with finality. "Sold to the lady for six dollars." An assistant carried the doll off.

The girls twisted around to get a look at the woman, but she was too far back to be seen. Ginnie turned to Geneva, who stared bleakly back at her. "Oh, I can't bear it," Geneva said.

"Why wasn't Miss Wade here!" Ginnie cried. "Or our mothers! It was Miss Wade's doll, I know it was. Wait till we tell her!" She paused. "Where do you suppose she's *been* all this time?"

Geneva shrugged helplessly.

"Geneva, don't you remember? Miss Wade said those people who rented her house lived in California. If they took her, how did Lady Vanderbilt get *here?*"

"I don't know." Geneva's eyes were on the auctioneer. "Look, we ought to watch what he's auctioning. We'll talk about it later." She settled round in her chair again. "I'm going to buy something, and nobody's going to stop me, so there!"

But everything was either uninteresting now or 'way beyond their reach. Ginnie would have bought an old school desk, but the price was too high from the start. At last Geneva bid for an old pitcher of quaintly flowered china and got it for a dollar. She handed the money over and accepted her prize with a look of huge relief. "Well, I got something, anyway. I'll give it to my mother," she said.

Ginnie was beginning to feel a little desperate. Two dollars were burning a hole in her pocket and she was willing to buy almost anything now rather than go away from the sale empty-handed. What was the good of going to an auction if you didn't buy something?

The auctioneer picked up a covered glass jar filled with something that Ginnie could not identify at once. He held the jar to the light, peering at it with interest.

"I have here buttons," he said. "Hundreds of good buttons from someone's old button box. Wonderful for any of you ladies who sew." He turned the jar intriguingly before his audience. "Who wants this fine stock of buttons?"

"Your mother sews a lot, Ginnie," Geneva remarked. "Why don't you get it?"

Ginnie hesitated. The buttons did not really interest her. But she did want to buy something, and suddenly, as the auctioneer held high the jar of buttons and no one spoke, Ginnie was surprised to hear her own voice. "Twenty-five cents."

"Twenty-five cents." The auctioneer looked around. "Anyone bid fifty? Going, going, sold for twenty-five cents to the young lady here!"

She had bought something. Ginnie handed over a quarter and accepted the jar, turning it to see the contents. Well, there seemed to be some pretty buttons in there along with a lot of ordinary ones. Sometime when she had nothing else to do it might be fun to look them all over and sort them out.

And then at last she heard her mother's voice. Mother and Mrs. Porter slid into the row and took the two empty seats.

"Mother!" Ginnie cried. "Guess what happened! We found Miss Wade's doll—the one she told us about! Only a woman bid higher than we did and she got her!"

"For goodness sake!" said Mother. "Are you sure it's the same doll? Have you spoken to the woman?"

"It's Lady Vanderbilt. We're sure. She's dressed exactly the same!" Geneva insisted.

"Where is the woman who bought her?" Mrs. Porter asked. "Let's talk to her."

They had not seen the bidder's face. "But we'll know her by the doll," Geneva said. "Come on, Ginnie, let's look for her."

There was no woman in the audience carrying an ancient doll in lavender taffeta. The girls wandered back to the last row of seats, scanning each row. Perhaps she put the doll under her chair, Ginnie thought, and she got down behind the last row and studied the ground under all the chairs. She saw some old butter molds, a footstool, a large platter, and some picture frames, but there was no Lady Vanderbilt.

Geneva had given up and was wandering back to her seat. Ginnie stood at the back of the crowd, looking around. Her eyes wandered toward the refreshment stand, the parking lot. . . .

Then she saw her. A young woman, slim and tanned, wearing white shorts and a plaid blouse, was just putting Lady Vanderbilt into the seat of a car. It was a red car, a small one. The Jaguar.

Wild excitement surged through Ginnie. I can catch her before she gets away, she thought. She started on the run.

Her path was blocked. Ginnie looked up at the

woman who had directed them when she and Geneva first came to the auction. "Did you find some nice things, dear?" The kind lady beamed down at her.

"Oh—yes. Thank you. I—we—would you please excuse me? I have to. . . ." Somehow she got around the solid obstacle in her way and headed for the parking lot.

But she was too late now. The red Jaguar was backing out of its parking spot. As Ginnie stood still, anguished, the car slipped smoothly down the drive to the road, turned away from town, and, carrying Lady Vanderbilt, quickly disappeared from sight.

CHAPTER 5

The Red Jaguar

"BUT Ginnie," Miss Wade protested, "surely it couldn't have been Lady V! Not after thirty years!"

"But it was, Miss Wade!" Ginnie insisted.

"You told us how she was dressed," Geneva pointed out, "and there couldn't be two dolls dressed just exactly like that. Could there?"

"I suppose not. She came from Paris. But the Lamberts—I always thought they. . . . Well, anyway," Miss Wade said, "where was she all that time and how in the world did she ever get into the auction?"

They were on Miss Wade's screened porch, where the girls had rushed to tell the news as soon as they got home. Mother and Mrs. Porter had come too, interested in this strange reappearance of the long-lost Lady V.

"I tried to find out where she came from," Mother said. "I asked a woman who seemed to be in charge, and she spoke to someone else. They said a Mrs. French had collected all the toys for the auction, and she'd be the only one who'd know where they came from. But she's left for North Carolina or someplace, and she'll be gone a month."

"That would be Mrs. Robert French," Miss Wade said. "She has a summer place. I don't know her except to speak to."

"It's a shame you didn't get up right away and speak to the woman who bought the doll," Mrs. Porter said to the girls.

"Oh, I know, I know!" Geneva moaned. "We just didn't think, we were so disappointed."

Ginnie put her head on one side, her forehead creased by the tiny wrinkle that always appeared when she was thinking hard. "I've got an idea," she said. "I bet we could find her."

"How?" Geneva demanded.

"Well, she's got a red Jaguar. If we went around looking for a red Jaguar, maybe we'd find her—and Lady V!"

"Good idea!" Geneva cried.

"Provided she's staying someplace around here," Mother said. "She probably is, since she went to the auction, but you never can tell."

"Let's start looking!" Ginnie exclaimed.

Miss Wade protested. "Why should you spend your lovely days on the Cape hunting for my old doll? After all. . . ."

"Oh, but we want to, Miss Wade!" Geneva assured her. "We're dying to find her."

"We saw her," Ginnie added, "and we loved her."

Miss Wade said quietly, "I loved her too."

Across Ginnie's mind those words from the diary—*Sh! It's a secret!*—flashed again, and she thought of the precious jewel. Lady V wasn't wearing any jewelry, I'm sure she wasn't, Ginnie thought. But of course she wouldn't still have the precious jewel. Who knew how many hands Lady

V had passed through, and what experiences she
had had.

It was on the tip of her tongue to say something
about the entry in the diary when Mother spoke
and the matter slipped Ginnie's mind.

"We can look around for the car," Mother said.
"But don't you want to go to the beach this afternoon and start hunting Jaguars tomorrow? It's
such a lovely day."

They decided they would go swimming, and
Ginnie raced Geneva home. She got into her bathing suit quickly. Going downstairs while Geneva
struggled with a broken lace in her sneaker, she
saw the jar of buttons and picked it up, unscrewing
the top. Idly she sat down and poured some of the
buttons upon the sofa, poking through them to see
what she had bought.

There were a few that were quite pretty, but
most of them were plain old yellowed buttons. She
could see nothing they might use on the pink dress
Mother was making her on her portable sewing
machine. Here was one old pinkish one, but it
was very dirty and the wrong shape. Ginnie gazed

at the odd-shaped button, smoothing it absently between thumb and finger, and sat thinking about the missing red Jaguar.

Geneva pounded downstairs. "I'm ready, come on!"

All afternoon, floating lazily on a rubber raft or lying on the sand as she watched the gulls come up over the dunes to meet the fishing boats, Ginnie thought about the mystery. Where, indeed, had Lady V been all those years? Even if they found the lady of the red Jaguar they would not know that.

There was a square dance in the town parking lot that night. Ginnie and Geneva formed a square with two small boys, a big sister and a little sister, and a father and daughter, while their mothers sat in the car and looked on. Between dances Ginnie wandered back into the darkness that the flood-lights did not reach, looking at the parked cars. But if the lady of the red Jaguar was anywhere in the vicinity, either she was not interested in square dancing or had something else to do this evening.

Next morning Mother said, "We've got to go

into town to do some marketing. Do you two sleuths want to come along and look for Jaguars?"

"Yes!" Ginnie said.

"We'll prowl around while you're in the store," Geneva added.

"Well, come on, Sherlock Holmes," Mother said.

As they turned into the main road Ginnie had another idea. "Mother!" she squealed into her mother's ear.

Mother stepped suddenly on the brake and turned, startled. "What's the matter?"

"I just had an idea!"

"Well, don't scare me to death even if you did have!"

Ginnie giggled and snuggled up. "I'm sorry."

"What's your idea?"

"We could stop at every gas station and ask if a red Jaguar comes there."

"Not such a bad idea at that," Mrs. Porter commented from the back seat.

"All right, let's try it." They were approaching a service station now, and Mother swung in. The attendant came out to meet them.

"Five gallons, please," Mother said, smiling at him. "And this young lady has a question to ask you."

Ginnie sat forward. "We want to know, please," she said, "whether anybody with a red Jaguar ever comes here to get gas."

The man gazed at her thoughtfully. "Don't think so, not lately. Not this year. There's more and more of these little foreign cars, but a Jag. . . . Wait a while now—there was one!"

"When?" Ginnie and Geneva spoke together, sitting bolt upright.

"That was a black one though."

"Oh." They sank back.

"Well, thank you anyway," Mother said, paying him. They went on their way.

Nor had the other gas station on the way into town seen anything of the car they were looking for. "It was a good idea anyway," Geneva consoled Ginnie.

"Only it didn't work," Ginnie said glumly.

They passed the dory full of petunias at Main and Commercial and drove slowly through Main Street, bustling and busy with shoppers this morning. Mother turned into the parking lot behind the town hall. The lot was filled with cars and it looked as if there weren't a single space available. Then Ginnie spied one. "There's an empty place, Mother," she said.

But the space was not vacant, as they saw in a moment. A red Jaguar was parked there.

For a minute they sat speechless, not believing their eyes. Then Ginnie said, "It can't be. It isn't!"

"But it is!" Geneva sang out. "Oh boy, oh boy, Ginnie, let's you and I stay right in this car and wait till she comes!"

Another car moved out then and Mother pulled into its place. "Now what are you going to do when you see this woman?" she inquired, picking up her handbag.

"Tell her she bought a long-lost doll and everything, and ask if we can show the doll to Miss Wade."

"All right, you stay here. We won't be gone long." Mother and Mrs. Porter left them.

They had a good view of the little red car. The two girls sat there, eyes glued to it. "Oh,

Ginnie, aren't you excited?" Geneva exclaimed.

"Yes." Ginnie was thoughtful. "But I'd certainly like to solve the mystery of where that Lady V has been!"

"So would I. But we probably won't," Geneva said philosophically.

"If those people—the Lamberts—took her," Ginnie persisted, "they must have left her someplace around here. Because how would she get back here from California? Only why would they take her and then leave her someplace?" She sighed deeply. "I just can't figure it out!"

Geneva had no answer. The girls sat quietly, their eyes on the red car and the other cars circling the parking lot and the women carrying bags of groceries. Every time a dark-haired young woman walked in from the street, the girls eyed her expectantly. Other cars pulled out and their places were taken. But no one came for the red Jaguar.

Absent-mindedly, Geneva began to sing one of the songs from last night's dance. *"You put your right foot in, you put your right foot out, you put your right foot in and you shake it all about....*

"She must be doing an awful lot of shopping or

something," she said impatiently, interrupting herself.

Ginnie's eyes idly followed a little fat man in white shorts as he pattered down the drive from the street and disappeared into the fish market. "Maybe she's at the beauty parlor."

"Well, we can't sit here all day. Whew, I'm hot!"

Ginnie was hot too, with the sun baking the metal top of the car and glinting off the hood. But she was determined. "Well, I'm going to stay till she comes," she said firmly.

After a while the little fat man came out with his fish. Ginnie watched him, without interest, as he came across the parking lot. He was heading for his car, of course.

"Oh, *no!*" Geneva cried suddenly.

Ginnie could not believe her eyes. The fat man was getting into the Jaguar.

Speechless with dismay, the girls watched him start the engine. The car moved easily out of its parking space.

"What's the matter?" Mother's voice said. Then her eyes followed their gaze. "Wasn't it your lady?"

"It was a little fat man!" Geneva cried in anguish.

"Oh, too bad!" Mrs. Porter exclaimed.

"Oh, I was so sure!" Ginnie moaned. "Unless," she cried suddenly, "it's her husband. Oh, he probably is! Mother, quick, let's follow him! Please!"

The mothers were putting their groceries into the car. "Oh, Ginnie!" Mother protested.

"Yes, yes, we've got to!" Geneva cried.

"All right." Mother climbed into the driver's seat and Mrs. Porter hastily slipped in beside Geneva. "If he hasn't disappeared," Mother added, backing the car quickly to circle the parking lot.

Both girls were sitting on the edge of their seats. "You look that way, Geneva, I'll look this," Ginnie said excitedly.

For a moment, as they paused at the exit and the traffic officer motioned them on, Ginnie saw nothing of the little red car. Then there was a brief flash of color through the trees and she cried, "There he is! I just saw him turn that corner up there! Hurry, hurry!"

Mother drove in pursuit of the car. At the corner there was no sign of the Jaguar, and the girls were desolate. They rounded the corner and came shortly to a fork. Mother slowed down. "Which way now?"

"Oh, I don't know, I don't know," Geneva moaned.

"Turn right," Ginnie said. "I don't know which way he went but turn right."

The right fork took them through pine woods, dotted with new-looking summer homes standing in their clearings. They crossed some railroad tracks and the road curved left. There was no red car in sight. At the end of the road Ginnie glimpsed the bay.

"Oh, I know where we are now!" she cried. They were approaching the Tecumseh Neck Road, slipping in by the back way. And, as they reached it, the red Jaguar suddenly shot across from the left just ahead of them.

Both girls screeched with joy. "Quiet!" Mrs. Porter admonished. "For goodness sake, you'll startle the natives!"

And now they were trailing the other car as it skimmed over the curving road, climbing along the narrow point that thrust into the bay. "He's turning," Mother said.

The Jaguar had its right direction signal on. It was slowing. Then it turned sharply into a driveway that led to an ultramodern house set high on a hillside. Mother slowed her car to a crawl.

"What do we do now?" Mrs. Porter asked.

"It's a little awkward to chase a man right up to his doorstep," Mother said.

"But we have to find out," Geneva wailed.

So in the end Mother turned into the drive. "Just go to the door, Ginnie," she said, "and tell them why you have come."

"I'll go too," Geneva volunteered.

It was the man himself who answered their ring. "How do you do?" he said courteously, a question in his voice.

"I—I'm sorry to bother you," Ginnie said, flurried. "But I—we—we're looking for somebody in a red car, like yours, a lady who bought a doll yesterday at the church auction."

He looked mystified. "A doll?"

"An old, old doll," Geneva explained.

The man shook his head. Then a thought

seemed to strike him and he said, "Just a moment, I'll ask my wife." He stepped away from the door and Ginnie felt little shivers of excitement run all over her. She looked at Geneva, the suspense almost unbearable.

He was coming back, and they could hear a feminine voice in the background. Then a lady appeared at the screen door.

She was short too, and quite as plump as her husband. She had a round, childlike face, frizzy fair hair, and blue eyes.

"Is there something I can do for you?" she said, smiling sweetly at the girls. "My husband didn't quite understand. Something about a doll?"

Ginnie gulped, disappointment taking her voice. She was relieved when she heard Geneva speaking. "Does any other lady ever drive your car?"

"No, indeed, no other lady ever drives my car," the blond woman told them firmly.

"Then—I guess there's some mistake," Geneva said. "It must have been somebody else—in another red Jaguar."

CHAPTER 6

Saturday

THERE appeared to be no clue to the where-abouts of a red Jaguar driven by a slim, dark-haired young woman. After the first shock of disappointment at the result of their wild-goose chase, Ginnie and Geneva giggled about the mistake they had made.

"She might not even be staying around here," Ginnie conceded with resignation.

"Oh, you'll probably run into her," Mother said.

"I can't bear it not to find Lady V!" Geneva declared passionately.

Meanwhile Miss Wade herself tried to find out who had given the doll to be auctioned, but her inquiries, like those of Ginnie's mother, faced an impasse. Only Mrs. French, visiting her daughter in North Carolina, knew where the dolls in the sale had come from.

One day the girls came home from the beach and saw Ernie cutting Miss Wade's grass. "Let's go over and talk to him," Ginnie suggested.

"You know what?" Geneva said. "He might know if there's another Jaguar around here."

They crossed the lawn in their bathing suits. "Hi, Ernie," Geneva called.

"Hi." As usual the boy did not seem too pleased to see them. He probably thinks we're too young to talk to, Ginnie decided philosophically.

"We want to ask you something, Ernie," Geneva said.

Ernie reluctantly paused in his mowing and drew an arm over his perspiring forehead.

"Do you know anybody around here who has a red Jaguar?" said Ginnie.

"Sure."

"Who?" the girls cried in unison.

"Mr. Thalheimer."

"Oh." Ginnie felt let down. "Where does he live?"

"Out Tecumseh Neck."

"We know him," Geneva said, disappointed. "Do you know anybody else—a lady?"

He scowled at them. "What's this all about?"

"A doll," Geneva said.

"A *what?*"

The girls giggled at his horrified expression. "Well, we'll tell you," Ginnie said. "There's this doll, a real old doll. She belonged to Miss Wade's mother, only she's been missing for years and years. But the other day at the church auction, there she was! And she was auctioned off and a lady bought her."

"So?" Ernie said scornfully, as if anything involving a ridiculous doll could not possibly merit a moment of his time.

"So we'd like to find the lady—she was driving a red Jaguar—and see if she would give Lady Vanderbilt back to Miss Wade."

"Lady. . . ." Ernie was staring at them, the queerest look on his face. Suddenly he glanced down at his arm, gave it a vicious slap, and studied it intently.

"What's the matter?" Geneva demanded.

"Measly gnats." Eyes still on his arm, Ernie said in a casual tone, "Did you say 'Lady Vanderbilt?' "

"That's the doll's name," Ginnie explained.

"Somebody stole her out of Miss Wade's attic years and years ago," Geneva related with relish. "We read about her in an old diary. Oh, and it said she had a precious jewel."

"A *what?*" Ernie said again, his eyes startled.

The girls laughed out loud at his astonishment. "A precious *jewel,*" Geneva repeated.

"Only that was in olden times, when Miss Wade's mother was a girl," Ginnie explained, taking pity on the boy's bewilderment. "Of course she hasn't got it now—the doll hasn't got the jewel, I mean. At least we don't think she has it, after all these years."

"What happened to it?" Ernie asked.

Geneva shrugged. "We don't know. We'd just like to find Lady Vanderbilt for Miss Wade. So if you see a red Jaguar besides the one that belongs to Mr.—whatever his name is—will you please let us know?"

"O.K.," Ernie said. "Look out, I got to get this grass cut now."

They trailed along after him as he cut a swath across the back yard. A car stood in the drive at the other side of Miss Wade's house. "Whose car is that?" Geneva asked.

"Mine. Why?"

She giggled. "It's so funny-looking!"

"It's a Model A Ford." Ernie paused, instantly defensive. "You don't find one of those every day. Perfect condition, too," he added grandly.

"It's nice and clean and shiny, Ernie," Ginnie said gently.

"It's O.K." The boy shrugged lightly. "I'm going to trade her in soon, though. Wait till you see the sports model I'm getting!" Ernie's eyes were suddenly bright with enthusiasm. Ginnie had never seen him look like that, and she gazed at the boy with interest. He looked different, lighted up inside.

"Are you really going to get a sports car?" Geneva asked curiously.

"Sure. When I get the money." Ernie's face broke into an impish grin which made it suddenly likable. Ginnie was intrigued by this new Ernie she was seeing for the first time. It was as if he had suddenly come to life. He really was car crazy, as Dr. Emerson had said.

"You like cars a lot, don't you?" she said.

All the expression drained out of his face, leaving it blank again, as if he suddenly realized he had shown too much of his feeling. "Yup," Ernie said briefly. He turned his lawn mower and headed in the other direction. Dismissed, the girls wandered homeward.

For the time being they put aside, reluctantly, the mystery of Lady Vanderbilt. Ginnie could not get the doll out of her mind, but there seemed to be nothing further they could do about it.

The summer days were slipping along now. Ginnie treasured every one. As the summer had advanced, a new world had come into being for her —the world at the edge of the sea. They had gone one night to an illustrated lecture on marine life, and after that Ginnie found books in the little library in the town hall and learned things she had never known about the tiny creatures of the water.

There were the barnacles. She knew now that the little gray incrustations covering the rocks were their shells, and that if she watched closely she might sometime see the barnacle itself reach out with its tentacles for food.

But some of the barnacle shells apparently had been abandoned, or else the barnacles had died, and in these snug little nests she could see minute snails, sometimes two or three, hardly larger than the tip of a pencil. How had they gotten into those barnacle shells on a rock that was far out of water at low tide? Had they climbed, with infinite slowness, the face of the rock? Or been washed in at high tide?

Perhaps they did climb the rock, for snails, or at least the whelk variety, could certainly get around. Wandering the beach at its deserted end, Ginnie came on what at first she thought were great beds of black pebbles. Then she discovered that they were living creatures—colonies of untold thousands of tiny whelks. Wherever the bay washed deeply into the beach, there was the long black trail of whelks. Ginnie never tired of crouching in the wet sand to watch the tiny snails move about, so slowly and smoothly, by means of one minute leg protruding from the shell.

Then there were the ridiculous, scurrying hermit crabs, always rushing crazily about under their clumsy shells in the shallow water. Ginnie was astonished to learn that they did not grow these shells but appropriated them, hunting until they found an empty whelk shell of the right size, discarding it when it became too small.

There were the periwinkle blue mussels, intertwined so toughly with the line of seaweed left by the tides. Ginnie loved the many-shaded greens and blues of the stones on the shore. Why was the sand sand-colored, she wondered, when the rocks were blue? And when she dug a toe into the wet sand close to the water, where shells abounded, the sand was indeed blue underneath, and the water that instantly seeped into the hollow had the color of indigo ink.

On the rare days when she did not get to the beach, at least for a walk along the sand, Ginnie felt restless and vaguely unhappy. She had the strange feeling that there, at the edge of the sea, she had discovered the heartbeat of life itself.

There were many things to do besides going to the beach. The girls had made their beach-plum jelly, firm and deepest crimson. Almost every week there was a church supper somewhere, or a food sale or auction. Now and then they watched a movie at the drive-in, and once there was a minstrel show in Eastham. They drove to Rock Harbor at ten o'clock one night to see the fishing boats come in on the tide and to watch the huge tuna being unloaded.

And almost every evening when the weather was fine they went for a drive. Tecumseh Neck was a good place from which to see the sunset, but Ginnie loved Rock Harbor, where the boats were black silhouettes against a crimson sky. And one night they happened on the loveliest sunset spot of all—a hilltop, quiet and serene, with a breathtaking view below of the little town and the harbor.

So each new day unfolded its own lovely pattern. Ginnie hugged every one to her heart.

Daddy and Mr. Porter arrived late Friday night for the weekend, and Ginnie and Geneva had plans to propose at breakfast.

"We want to go to the back side to swim," Geneva announced, using with relish the native term for the ocean side of the Cape. "And we want to have a lobster supper on the beach, maybe at New-comb Hollow."

"And Daddy," Ginnie said, "could we go exploring on some back roads? I just love back roads!"

"And we'd like to go to a buffet supper someplace on Sunday," Geneva announced. "Lots of restaurants have buffet suppers Sunday. A girl at the beach said they had *super* things to eat—lobster and shrimp and chicken salad and *everything!* And you can eat all you want!"

"Anything else you've arranged?" Mr. Porter asked meekly.

"We want to show you the sunset from our secret place," Ginnie cried.

"Would you mind saving a couple of projects for Daddy's vacation?" Mrs. Porter asked her child.

"Why don't we have the ocean swim and the beach picnic this afternoon anyway?" Mother suggested. "We can't go to any buffet supper tomorrow, because Daddy and Mr. Porter have to start back by midafternoon."

Geneva and her parents decided to drive to Harwich that morning to call on some friends, so

Ginnie, Mother, and Daddy took this time for exploring.

They took the old King's Highway toward Truro. It was always hard for Ginnie to decide which she loved most—the woodsy roads in the hollows, cool with shadows and warm with the scent of pine, or the winding trails over the open moors. But this morning, when the road topped the billowing moors and Ginnie saw the green hills of Truro, with their white spires, and the shimmering mist-blue bay beyond, she begged her father to stop.

"Oh, isn't it beautiful!" she cried. "I want to get out, Daddy!"

The wind from the sea, always blowing, held all the rich scents of the moors. Ginnie picked a bouquet of beach plums and bay. When she climbed back into the car, she crushed a handful of the bay leaves and sniffed ecstatically of their aromatic fragrance as they drove on.

They took side roads to beaches they had never visited before, and followed the Truro roads, which never seemed to go anywhere except back where they started, up and down the wooded hills.

Daddy said at last that they had explored all
there was up this way. Ginnie was satisfied. Now
she was ready for an afternoon on the beach.

They were halfway back when they saw Ernie.
His Model A was parked at the side of the road, its
hood up. Ernie was intently tinkering with the
engine.

Daddy stopped the car. "Having trouble?" he
called out.

Quickly Ernie looked up, the proud color flam-
ing into his face as he recognized them. He wiped
the back of an oil-stained hand over his forehead.
"A little," he admitted reluctantly.

Daddy got out and went over to the other car.
"What seems to be the matter?"

"I think I need a new part," Ernie said, his dis-
comfiture at his predicament evident. "I'll have
to leave her here."

"Where are you headed?"

"House up the road—about a mile."

"Shall we take you there?" Daddy asked, "or do
you want to go back to town?"

Ernie gazed at the road to town, which looked,
Ginnie thought, cooler and shadier than the hot

sunny trail in the opposite direction. He hesitated, then gave a small sigh. "I'd better get up there— if you don't mind. I'm supposed to fix some window they can't open. But you'd have to turn around," he said suddenly. "I can walk. . . ."

"Nonsense," Daddy said. "Get in, son."

"Hi, Ernie," Ginnie greeted him.

"Hi." He climbed into the back seat, carrying a bag of tools.

"Is it one of the houses your mother looks after?"

"That's right."

He's embarrassed, Ginnie thought. He told us his car was in perfect condition, and now it has broken down.

They dropped him at a house high on a hill, with a long drive winding up to it. "This is O.K., right here," he said. "Thanks."

"Can you get a lift back to town?" Daddy asked.

"Oh, sure."

As they turned around he went toiling up the road to the house in the glaring sun. Somehow Ginnie knew that Ernie was hot with humiliation, too.

"Poor kid," Mother said with a rueful little laugh.

"Poor Ernie," Ginnie echoed. "He works hard. I wonder if he ever gets a chance to go swimming."

"That reminds me," Mother said. "We must go around by the town pier and order the lobsters."

Ginnie and her father went into the little shack, which smelled so strongly of boiling lobster, and Ginnie watched the handsomely colored creatures swimming in their tank while Daddy gave the order.

They drove slowly back up Commercial Street. "Oh!" Mother exclaimed suddenly. "Potato chips! And I think we need coffee. Let me out here before you go into the parking lot."

Ginnie got out too. But instead of going into the store she strolled on past it to see if anything exciting was posted on the bulletin board.

There were the usual things—a church supper in Brewster, some rooms to let, fishing parties. . . .

Something seemed to be going on at the Historical Society. People were milling about the lawn. Ginnie looked to see if Mother was coming, but since there was no sign of her she went over to investigate.

It was an art exhibit. The pictures were set up on the lawn, and although Ginnie was not too interested in pictures she wandered past the display, looking them over. Many were seascapes or studies of old Cape Cod scenes; others were still lifes. There were one or two moderns that she studied with a little frown. She did not understand why grownups painted pictures that children could do just as well.

Here was a picture she was pleased to recognize as Nauset Light from its band of strong red. She moved on to the next canvas.

And suddenly Ginnie froze. She stared at the picture before her for an unbelieving moment. Then she gave a gasp and looked wildly around. She saw her father, who had strolled over from the car.

"Daddy!" she called. "Quick! Come here!"

It was a portrait of Lady V. Regal in lavender taffeta, sweeping train, and lace fichu, the doll smiled serenely out of the canvas at Ginnie.

CHAPTER 7

Lost Lady V

"SO that is the lost Lady Vanderbilt," Daddy said.

"Oh," Ginnie cried, "I wish Geneva were here!"

She looked up and suddenly, as if by some miracle, Geneva was there. She and Mrs. Porter and Mother were all walking up the street together.

"Hi, Ginnie!" Geneva called gaily. "We stopped to get potato chips and your mother stopped to get potato chips."

"Oh, Geneva!" Ginnie ran to meet them. "Mother, Mrs. Porter, guess what! There's a picture of Lady V here!"

"A *what?*" Geneva stood still and stared at her.

"Hurry, hurry, I'll show you!"

They all stood in front of the portrait, gazing in silence at the queenly Lady Vanderbilt. Then

Mother said, "Who painted it?" and stooped to read the artist's name, signed in the corner. "It looks like *Joseph Jeffries*."

"Where's Dr. Emerson?" Mrs. Porter asked. "He might know who the artist is."

"How did Joseph Jeffries get into this?" Geneva demanded.

"We'll find out," her mother said, and went off to look for the curator. She brought Dr. Emerson back.

"We are very anxious to find the artist who painted this picture," she told him. "Can you tell us anything?"

Dr. Emerson looked over his glasses at the canvas and bent to examine the signature. Then he straightened with a smile. "Ah, yes," he said, apparently pleased. "Indeed I can. It happens that this artist is a former college student of mine. Does very nicely, don't you think? For someone who never painted until a couple of years ago?"

"But when did he paint this picture?" Ginnie asked, bewildered.

"Where *is* he?" Geneva demanded. "We have to see him!"

The old gentleman looked puzzled. He bent again to make sure of the name. "This artist is a young woman."

"His name's Joseph!" Geneva cried.

"Ah, I see! Of course. No, her name is Josepha. Josepha Jeffries. Married name, that is. Her name when I had her as a student. . . ."

"Oh, where is she, Dr. Emerson?" Geneva cried. "Please tell us!"

An idea burst upon Ginnie. "Does she have a red Jaguar?" she cried, and held her breath.

Dr. Emerson turned first to Geneva. "Mrs. Jeffries is in a studio cottage on White Sands Road, about a mile out." He bowed in Ginnie's direction. "My dear young lady, yes, she does have a red Jaguar."

"Oh-h!" Ginnie and Geneva collapsed into each other's arms in the sheer, unbelievable joy of discovery.

"Oh, please, Mother, let's go right up there!" Ginnie begged.

Mother laughed, shaking her head apologetically at Dr. Emerson. "This is a long story," she told him. "We've been hunting for Mrs. Jeffries.

We'll have to tell you about it some other time, but thank you so much for helping us find her at last."

"She's been staying in Provincetown with a friend," the old gentleman said. "Just got into her place here yesterday. Expects her husband up in a couple of weeks, I believe. He is serving in the Navy."

"That's why we couldn't find her," Ginnie said with a deep sigh of enlightenment.

They thanked Dr. Emerson again. As they walked back to the cars Mother said, "I think Miss Wade should be the one to call on Mrs. Jeffries. We can't all go over there. Suppose we go home and tell her."

But when Ginnie and Geneva raced breathlessly across the lawn, Miss Wade's door was locked. They pounded, unable to believe that at this crucial moment in their search for the lost Lady V Miss Wade had failed them. At last they turned slowly homeward, the disappointment almost unbearable.

"Her car's out," Ginnie said, glancing toward the garage.

Mother said, "She's probably gone to the store."

"No." Geneva shook her head. "She doesn't lock the door when she just goes to the store."

They had lunch, but Ginnie found it hard to swallow food. She was afire with impatience. Her mother reached across the table and patted her hand. "Calm down, darling. Of course you're anxious to see this Mrs. Jeffries, but now we know where she is, so a day won't matter. She'll be there."

"I know." Ginnie could not have told why she felt this strong sense of urgency about getting to Lady V. She gave a troubled sigh.

"We're going to Newcomb Hollow this afternoon, anyway," Mrs. Porter reminded her. "You still want to go, don't you?"

"Sure she does!" Geneva cried. "Come on, let's get ready, Ginnie. We can see Miss Wade tomorrow."

There was no sign of Miss Wade when they drove away, and gradually, as the afternoon passed, the exhilaration of battling the breakers distracted Ginnie's mind from the other excitement.

At five, Mr. Porter and Daddy picked up the

boiled lobsters, one for each. They ate them with melted butter and potato chips and whole ripe red tomatoes, and had watermelon, crisp and sweet, for dessert.

The beach was deserted now. The sea breeze turned cool, and in the western sky the opalescent colors of sunset began to stain the clouds. "Where's this secret sunset place?" Daddy asked.

So the day ended on Ginnie's hilltop. They looked down on the harbor, the little boats asleep in their marina, and the tranquil white village set in its green hollow. Sunset flooded the west. And at seven o'clock the sweet sound of church bells floated through the clear, still air.

The afternoon had calmed and relaxed Ginnie. That sense of fierce urgency was gone, although she looked forward eagerly to seeing Miss Wade in the morning, perhaps even tonight. But, as they drove up, the windows of the house next door were blank and dark.

"She still isn't home!" Geneva complained. "Where *is* she?"

And instantly a little edge of uneasiness stirred uncomfortably somewhere deep inside Ginnie.

In the morning they overslept, and when they finally ran over to Miss Wade's house Miss Wade had her hat on, ready to go to church.

"Where were you last night, Miss Wade?" Geneva cried accusingly.

"Gallivanting," Miss Wade said gaily. "I was invited out to the Melody Tent and dinner. What do you think of that? Why are you two young ones panting with excitement?"

She listened to their story wonderingly.

"Why girls, how perfectly weird! A portrait! Why, I can't wait to see this young lady. Only...." She frowned. "The minister is coming to dinner. I can't possibly do it today." She saw their faces fall. "We'll go tomorrow without fail."

There was nothing for Ginnie to do but curb her impatience and wait.

So Daddy and Mr. Porter left, and it was Monday morning, the beginning of a new week, clear and dewy fresh, with the chickadees calling from the trees. The girls were about to head for Miss Wade's when they saw a car full of strange people drive up. Their neighbor had unexpected guests. It was more than a human being should be asked to endure, Ginnie thought. She went back into the house and threw herself face down on the sofa with a little moan.

After a while she sat up, gave a deep sigh, and looked about for some time-passing occupation. Geneva and her mother had gone off somewhere. The jar of buttons stood on the table and Ginnie slid disconsolately down on the floor and shook out some of the contents, absent-mindedly matching them up. Here were two brass buttons that went together, and three rather homely red ones, and a whole bunch of plain old white buttons, and four yellow ones. Here was that odd, dirty pink one that seemed to have no mates. She poked through, trying to find another like it, then swept the lot back into the jar, bored, and wandered outdoors.

She decided to go for a walk. Perhaps some more blackberries were ripe in that patch beyond Miss Wade's house. Ginnie wandered along the road, stopping to pick a bouquet of blue chicory and Queen Anne's Lace.

The flowers were all different now, she thought, snapping stems. The strong white daisies and handsome brown-eyed Susans and tiger lilies of

July were gone, and in their place were purple clover and crimson beach plums and the purplish leaves of the blueberry bushes. Everywhere bouncing Bet—old maid's pinks, Miss Wade called it—had replaced the delicate wild roses. And the wild cranberries covering the ground gleamed scarlet among their well-groomed, waxy green leaves. She walked on, pausing to gather a brilliant cluster of orange butterfly weed.

Birds sang close about her. "Chick-a-dee-dee-dee!" "Phee-be! Phee-be!" Like the daisies and brown-eyed Susans, the bobwhite seemed to have departed.

Geneva came back and the two girls waited with mounting impatience. Miss Wade's friends took her out to lunch. It was three-thirty when they brought her back and the girls saw the car drive away at last.

"I'm sorry," Miss Wade apologized when they went over. "There wasn't a thing I could do about it. Now come on, we're going to see your Mrs. Jeffries!"

Miss Wade was familiar with White Sands Road. "I know those cottages," she said. "There's quite a group of them on Innes Inlet, 'way back in the woods. She's probably in that remodeled apartment over the garage.''

White Sands Road was literally white sand, hardly more than a trail leading off a secondary paved road that wound down toward the bay. Miss Wade drove cautiously, for there was no place here to pass a car. But they met no one, and shortly they emerged into a wide clearing with the sparkle of blue water visible through the trees. The garage, with its wide-windowed apartment above, stood nearest them. There was a glimpse of another cottage some distance away, apparently directly on the water, and as Miss Wade brought the car to a halt the sound of voices drifted from that direction. Several cars were parked at the far side of the clearing. It sounded as if a party was in progress.

"Her car isn't here," Ginnie said anxiously, glancing in at the empty garage.

"I bet she's out!" Geneva exclaimed tragically.

Even as she spoke, a woman appeared from among the trees at the far side of the clearing, where the cars stood. She stopped for a moment, apparently calling back to someone.

"There she is!" Ginnie exclaimed excitedly. "That's the woman I saw at the auction, that's the one!"

Mrs. Jeffries came toward them. Suddenly they saw her stop and stand still, gazing in their direction. Then she quickened her pace almost to a run. "What's she running for?" Geneva demanded.

Mrs. Jeffries was acting strangely. She hurried toward them, and as she came closer Ginnie could see that her face wore an expression of extreme concern. She had almost reached them when she stood still again, gazing all around as if searching for something.

"What's the matter with her?" Ginnie said, mystified.

Miss Wade got out of the car as Mrs. Jeffries came nearer. "Mrs. Jeffries?" she said. "I am Allison Wade. I'm sorry to bother you, but. . . ."

"Excuse me." Mrs. Jeffries broke in quickly. "I am so upset!" She put a slim brown hand to her throat. "My car seems to have been stolen!"

It was a shock. "It couldn't have been stolen!" Miss Wade said after a moment, incredulous.

"Where is it?" Mrs. Jeffries waved her arm. "It was here, right in front of the cottage, and it's gone!" She pushed back her dark hair with a distracted gesture. "I—I'd better call the police. If I can get to a telephone. . . ."

"We'll take you." Miss Wade moved toward the car and opened the rear door. "Hop in. There's a gas station close by on the highway. You can call from there."

Then, when she had turned the car and they were groping along the sand trail again, Miss Wade said, "Now what happened? Tell us."

"I went over to Mrs. Newell's. She has that white house on the water and she had some people in this afternoon. I left the car outside my cottage. The key was in the ignition—oh, wasn't that foolish! But I never thought—'way back here in the woods!"

"And you were just coming back from the party?"

"I ran back for a minute to get. . . ." Mrs. Jeffries stopped short. From the front seat Ginnie heard her give a small gasp and, with a feeling of premonition, her heart leaped suddenly to her throat.

"She was in the car!" Mrs. Jeffries exclaimed.

"Who was?" Geneva asked.

"Oh, a doll. I left her in the car. I wanted to show her to someone. That's why I ran home."

Ginnie was conscious of her own sharply indrawn breath, and she and Geneva stared at one another. After a moment Geneva said in a flat voice, "That's why we came."

Her mind on her loss, Mrs. Jeffries did not seem to hear.

"Never mind now, girls," Miss Wade murmured, watching the road. "She has enough on her mind. Don't bother her." Over her shoulder she said to Mrs. Jeffries, "I'll explain later how we happened to come to see you. It was about the doll. We saw the painting you did and—well, you bought the doll at the auction, didn't you?"

"Yes."

"I can tell you something about her history," Miss Wade said quietly, "later."

"I'd love to hear it." Mrs. Jeffries was courteous but only half attending. "Right now I'm so distracted about the car. . . ."

"Of course you are. Here's the gas station."

They turned in. "You go and report to the police and we'll wait for you."

They watched her, trim and attractive in her blue shirtwaist dress and straw sandals. Then Ginnie spoke quickly. "Geneva, let's get out a minute."

Out of range of Miss Wade's hearing she said in a low voice, "Geneva, I'm just bursting!"

"What do you mean?"

"Lady Vanderbilt has disappeared *again!*"

Geneva frowned, shaking her head. "Ginnie, she just happened to be in the car. Don't get so excited."

"Or maybe," Ginnie said deliberately, "somebody stole the car because she was in it!"

Geneva stared at her for a moment. "That's silly. Why didn't they just take the doll?"

"I don't know. But it's mysterious. First Lady V pops up and then she disappears again. Maybe it isn't a jewel or anything like that, but. . . ."

"Here she comes," Geneva said warningly.

Mrs. Jeffries was looking relieved. "I got the chief of police," she said, as they all climbed back into the car. "He said they would get busy at once and not to worry, because whoever took the car couldn't get off the Cape. That's the silly part of it!" She shook her head. "How could anyone hope to get away with a red Jaguar!"

"Maybe we can find it!" Geneva said suddenly.

"Oh, Miss Wade," Ginnie cried, "couldn't we please drive around and look?"

Miss Wade hesitated. "I wouldn't have the faintest idea where to look."

"I don't want to take your time," Mrs. Jeffries protested. "I haven't even asked how you happened to come to see me. How rude can I be! And I'm so grateful to you. You said—the doll?"

"Later. It's a long story," Miss Wade told her. "We came because we saw the picture. I have a special interest in that doll, but that can wait."

"A very special interest," Geneva said dramatically.

"Well, I had too," Mrs. Jeffries said. "She reminded me of—something."

But Mrs. Jeffries' mind was on her car, and she kept peering down the road. The girls obeyed Miss Wade's instructions not to discuss the matter for the time being.

"Whoever took the car," Miss Wade was saying, "either headed right for the highway—in which case it's up to the police—or turned down toward the bay."

"You know all the back roads," Ginnie reminded her.

"Not all of them." Miss Wade drove slowly past White Sands Road. There were many trails through the woods here, leading to summer colonies and cottages, and she slowed at each one so they could look through the trees for a glimpse of a red car.

"I suppose someone could hide a car in a garage and try to get it out at night," Mrs. Jeffries remarked.

Now they were at the water. The road ended in a sandy turn-around and Miss Wade swung the car about and headed back. They had almost reached White Sands Road again when Ginnie said, "There was a road that went off back there, Miss Wade. We just passed it. Could we go down there?"

"I didn't see a road." But Miss Wade reversed

the car and backed. "That? That's hardly a trail, Ginnie."

"I know, but if they didn't head for the highway they had to go *somewhere*. We didn't pass any other road."

Miss Wade looked doubtful, but she turned the car into the weed-grown sand ruts for a short exploration. "It doesn't look as if it goes anywhere."

The girls sat on the edge of the front seat, anxious eyes on the road. The trail meandered through a patch of flat, open moorland and the sand was not deep, so the going was easy enough. But a patch of pine woods lay ahead and Miss Wade began to be nervous. "I don't think there's any use. . . ." she began.

"No. Don't go any farther," Mrs. Jeffries begged. "Please turn around here."

Suddenly Ginnie exclaimed, "Well! It must go somewhere—because look! See those tire tracks? Some car's been in here!"

They all saw them then, and Geneva said, "Ginnie, let's run ahead and find out where it goes."

"I'll go too," Mrs. Jeffries said. "It must go

either to a dump or some house. Come on, we'll investigate and then we'll feel better. We'll be right back," she assured Miss Wade.

The three set off up the trail. Almost immediately it entered the woods and curved toward the bay, and then, to Ginnie's surprise, she saw that the road did not end but began to climb, running parallel to the shore.

The sand ruts were deeper now, running between steep banks covered with wild cranberry, and the pine woods came thickly down to the narrow trail.

"It's a good thing Miss Wade didn't drive in here," Mrs. Jeffries said. "She couldn't have turned around. How much farther do you suppose this goes?"

Where the road went they never learned. Geneva, walking ahead, suddenly stood stock-still. Ginnie almost ran into her. Geneva's eyes were fixed ahead. Then Ginnie and Mrs. Jeffries saw it too. Ahead of them the road widened. It was still not wide enough for Miss Wade's car to turn, but there was space for a small car to swing about.

Standing in the turn-out, headed in the opposite direction, was the red Jaguar.

Mrs. Jeffries was running toward her car, hastily inspecting it. "It seems to be all right," she said quickly. "Oh, thank goodness!"

"Is the key there?" Geneva asked, coming up.

"Yes, the keys are here."

Ginnie was standing by the red car, peering in. It was the first time she had had a chance to inspect a car like this at close range. It seemed strange to be looking at last at the red Jaguar they had hunted so long.

One thing was wrong, though. Ginnie was not surprised. Except for the queer jolt it gave her to realize she had been right.

Lady Vanderbilt was nowhere to be seen.

CHAPTER 8

In the Sand

GINNIE lay on her back in the sand, Mother's straw beach hat over her face. As she gazed through it at the sky, every tiny hole in the varicolored straw became a rainbow—a strong band of red, then orange, yellow, green, and blue shading into violet.

It was just ten o'clock and they were almost the only people on the beach, but they wanted to make up for the day they had missed yesterday. Under the green-and-white umbrella Mother and Mrs. Porter leaned against their back rests and chatted. Honey panted softly, watching over them all.

Geneva gave a grunt and sat up restlessly. "I'd like to know how detectives solve mysteries!" she said. "They always have clues and stuff. We haven't got a single clue!"

Ginnie turned her head to one side under the hat. "We've solved some of it, Geneva. We found Lady Vanderbilt at the auction, and then we found Mrs. Jeffries, and then we found the Jaguar."

"That's not *solving*. We haven't one single idea who took the car, or where Lady V is now. Or where she was all those years, either." Geneva played with the sand, absent-mindedly scooping it into soft little mounds.

Ginnie pushed herself up and sat gazing reflectively out over the calm water. A speedboat hummed across the bay, its wake a feathery, arching plume of spray. One early sailboat dipped against the azure sky.

Geneva demolished her sand hill with an impatient swoop and flopped onto her stomach. "Let's go over the whole thing."

"What do you mean?"

"From the beginning. Everything that's happened to Lady V. Maybe we'll get a clue."

"O.K." Good idea, Ginnie thought, to get things sorted out. Besides, she loved anything resembling a story. "I'll begin," she offered with relish. "Once, many years ago, there was a girl. And her uncle was a sea captain and he sailed all over the world. And one time he brought her a beautiful doll from Paris, named Lady Vanderbilt. And then she wrote down in her diary that her doll had a precious jewel, but it was a secret."

Ginnie paused, rolling the idea of the secret jewel about in her mind, going back for a moment to her early theory that there was some connection between the jewel and the doll's first disappearance.

"Go on," Geneva prompted.

Ginnie continued. "Many years went by. The girl got married and had a daughter—that's Miss Wade. And when she was an old lady she died— not Miss Wade, her mother. And the doll was in the attic. And Miss Wade went to Europe and rented her house to some people."

"Named Lambert," Geneva contributed.

"Lambert. And when Miss Wade got home— well, after she'd been home quite a while—she happened to look for the doll and she was gone. So she was pretty sure the Lamberts had taken her. They had some children, I forgot to say. Only she didn't want to blame it on them, and anyway they had gone back to California. So she didn't do anything about it."

"And the *next* time she saw the doll. . . ." Geneva went on dramatically.

"She hasn't seen her yet!" Ginnie reminded her. "Where was I? Oh yes, many years later Lady Vanderbilt—that was the doll's name—was auctioned off at the church auction and Mrs. Jeffries, who is an artist, bought her."

"Why did she buy her? Just so she could paint the picture?" Geneva inquired.

"I guess so. Oh yes, and she said Lady V reminded her of something. We didn't ask her what she reminded her of."

"No," Geneva complained, "because Miss Wade hurried us right home after we found the car."

Mrs. Jeffries had gone directly to the police station, so there had been no chance to talk to her about the doll. However, Miss Wade had promised they could go over and see her today.

"Well, anyway," Ginnie went on, "after Mrs. Jeffries bought the doll, she painted her picture while she was visiting a friend in Provincetown. And then she moved into a studio on White Sands

Road, and she put the picture in an exhibition. And then she left the keys in her car one day and somebody stole the car!"

"And *also* Lady V!"

"And we found the car. Only Lady V wasn't in it!" Ginnie concluded.

They were both silent, watching the myriad twinklings of sunshine on the water.

"So there are two mysteries," Geneva said slowly, after a few moments. "First, where was Lady V all those years and how did she get back to Cape Cod if the Lamberts took her to California? Second, who stole her out of Mrs. Jeffries' car? And why?"

"There's really another mystery, Geneva," Ginnie said, a bit defensively. "About the jewel. Because if there really was a jewel once, what became of it?"

"Miss Wade must know. Probably she's got it. All we have to do is ask her, only you won't. You're stubborn."

Ginnie sighed. "I thought it might be part of the mystery—about her disappearing and everything—and we could solve it."

"Well, we haven't solved anything yet. Maybe the police will if they find Lady V." Geneva got to her feet. "I'm too hot to live. Come on in the water."

They raced each other, splashing into the water and plunging under the frothy coolness. As they walked back to their place on the beach later, Ginnie stooped to pick up a scallop shell.

"Look," she called after Geneva, "this is a real live scallop."

She placed the scallop on the sand near her beach jacket, arranged her towel, and stretched out on it. She and Geneva were quiet for a few minutes, enjoying the hot sun on their cold, wet bodies and breathing hard after their plunge. When Ginnie opened her eyes she was surprised to see that the scallop shell, tightly closed before, was slightly open. As she watched, it opened farther.

"Sst!" Ginnie said, making a quick gesture. Honey barked sharply. The shell closed with a snap and Ginnie laughed out loud. For a while she and Geneva made a game of being very still while the scallop cautiously peered out of his house. At the slightest move he banged the shell shut.

"He's smart," Ginnie said affectionately. "And he's cute. I'm going to take him home. I'll get some water." She carried her cap to the water, filled it, and placed the shellfish in it. "Now you

can breathe," she said. "Let's take a walk, Geneva."

The tide was so high this morning that the great rock was completely under water. They had to run up on the sandy, grassy bank to round the point and then keep close to the bluff. Here the water was ankle-deep and warm, and Ginnie liked the feel of the resilient sand beneath.

She kept her eyes on the clear water. A sand crab, swimming upright with waving claws, sank silently beneath the sandy bottom as she bent over, vanishing so completely that Ginnie could hardly believe she had seen him. Hermit crabs rushed clumsily about. Ginnie cupped her hands about one and lifted him out of the water. Instantly he retreated into his house, only his tiny, curled-up legs showing. When she put him back, the shell turned over, rocking the tiny creature in the waves like a cradle.

They sauntered along. Ginnie put a foot into the quivering pink-and-green froth left by the tide, and rainbow bubbles ran away like quicksilver. Honey sniffed happily on business of his own. Ginnie stood still at last and lifted her eyes from the shallows. They had come a long way.

It was a still morning. On this part of the beach, which was hidden from the bathing beach, there were no sounds but the faint hypnotic buzz of the speedboat—almost unseen out on the bay—and the light lapping of the water. Not a whisper stirred in the reeds. The wind, usually so violent in assaulting Ginnie's eardrums, had dropped.

Geneva flopped down on the grassy bank. "Let's rest a while."

"All right. We've walked miles." Ginnie sat down beside her with a sigh of contentment and gazed out on the bay. "Oh, I adore walking along the beach and seeing. . . ."

She started suddenly. Something had rustled in the reeds above their heads. Honey raised his head and barked, eyes alert.

"What was that?" Geneva demanded, stiffening.

"Maybe it was a rabbit."

"I hope it wasn't a snake!" Geneva scrambled to her feet and looked so horrified at the thought that Ginnie laughed.

"There aren't any snakes here!"

"I hope not!"

"Maybe it was just the wind," Ginnie said. But she looked out over the bay as she spoke, and the sail on the little boat hung limp.

A slight, undefinable chill had crept over their spirits. They sat there, silent. The only sound was a car starting, somewhere in the distance. A drifting cloud darkened the sun and the bay, so sparkling a moment before, seemed suddenly gray and forbidding. For a moment Ginnie had the strange sensation that she and Geneva were alone in a hostile world. She could scarcely believe that just beyond that point was the safe, familiar beach. Were Mother and Mrs. Porter really there?

Suddenly she wanted to get back. "Come on," she said, and got to her feet, starting along the narrow strip of sand.

Afterward it seemed to Ginnie the strangest thing that had ever happened to her. For the thought of Lady Vanderbilt came into her mind. She had not been thinking of her at all, not since they had started their walk along the beach. But now, quite unbidden, the thought was there.

So when Honey nuzzled something with particular interest and she saw the doll, lying in plain sight in the sandy reeds on the bluff, it seemed perfectly natural. She stooped and picked her up, and heard Geneva's gasp behind her. Only then did Ginnie come to her senses. She stood holding the doll, staring.

"I can't believe it!" Geneva cried. "We've found

her, Ginnie! And we weren't even looking! Where did she *come* from? Let me see her!"

The stately doll was sandy, but otherwise she appeared unhurt. This was the first time since the hurried moments at the auction that they had actually seen her, yet Lady Vanderbilt seemed like an old and beloved friend now.

"Oh, where have you been?" Ginnie murmured, holding her close and gazing into the smiling eyes.

"What wicked person left you on the beach?" Geneva exclaimed. "Ginnie, let's hurry. Oh, I can't wait to show Mother! Let's go straight up to Mrs. Jeffries' house!"

"Or should we take her to Miss Wade?" Ginnie wondered.

"I don't know. I'm too excited! Come on, Ginnie!"

They had no time now to speculate on how Lady Vanderbilt came to be on the beach or what strange chance had led them to her. They had Lady V. That was enough.

Mother and Mrs. Porter were excited too. They exclaimed over the beautiful old doll and Mother

said, "I can't undersand it at all! This is completely mystifying."

"It doesn't make sense," Mrs. Porter argued. "Somebody brought her down here and left her? *Why?* And then you girls stumble right on her? I don't believe it!"

Sense or no sense, Ginnie held the lost Lady V tightly in her arms. "Oh, Geneva, will you bring my pet scallop? No, put him back in the bay for me, please." She had more important matters to take care of now. Excitedly they all gathered their belongings and trooped up to the car.

"Let me hold her, Ginnie," Geneva begged, and Ginnie transferred her gently to Geneva's arms. They both looked the doll over carefully. Lady Vanderbilt, Ginnie saw, was wearing no jewelry.

They drove straight to Mrs. Jeffries' house. "Perhaps she'll let you take the doll home to show Miss Wade," Mother said.

But there was no sign of the red Jaguar as they drove into the clearing. "Oh, I hope she isn't out," Ginnie moaned softly. "Is her car in the garage?"

The Jaguar was not in the open garage. But another car stood there. And suddenly Ginnie exclaimed, "Why, that looks like Ernie's car!"

"Ernie's?" Geneva sounded incredulous. "What would he be doing here?"

"Go up and knock at the door, Ginnie," Mother suggested.

She climbed the steps to the apartment and knocked, a bit timidly, her heart pounding. At first there was no response. She waited, then knocked again.

Someone was coming. Someone was turning the knob inside. The door opened—reluctantly, it seemed to Ginnie.

Then she was staring at Ernie, and he was looking back at her. Ernie was scowling, as if she were annoying him as usual. But there was another expression in his eyes, and suddenly Ginnie thought, He's frightened. Ernie is frightened of something.

Just as quickly the wondering thought came, But he couldn't be frightened of *me!*

CHAPTER 9

Part of the Puzzle

"WHAT are you doing here?" said Ernie curtly.

He took the words out of Ginnie's mouth and automatically she echoed them. "What are *you?*"

"Fixing the faucet."

After a moment the explanation dawned on her. "Oh, is your mother the agent for this house, too?"

"Sure she is."

Mother called then. "Ginnie, ask Ernie to come down here for a minute."

The boy hesitated, then reluctantly he emerged and came down the stairs behind Ginnie. "I've got work to do," he muttered. But he came over to the car, civil enough.

"Hello, Ernie, how are you?" Mother said. "I

take it this is one of the houses you and your mother look after?"

"That's right."

"You never told us!" Geneva cried accusingly.

"Told you what?"

In the surprise of finding him here, both Ginnie and Geneva had forgotten for the moment that they had not talked to Ernie since they had learned who the buyer of the doll was. "You said you didn't know where there was a red Jaguar!"

"Geneva—gently," Mrs. Porter admonished, but the mothers were interested too.

"I didn't," Ernie said. "I hadn't even been up here. I didn't know who had the place."

"She didn't move in till later," Ginnie recalled.

"Anyway," Mother said, "where is Mrs. Jeffries, Ernie? Do you know?"

He did not know. She had called yesterday and asked to have a new washer installed in the kitchen faucet, but she had not been here when he came this morning.

"Well, remember the doll we told you about?" Ginnie said. "We found out Mrs. Jeffries was the one who bought her."

"Only somebody stole her again," Geneva went on. "Do you know about the car being stolen?"

"I heard. She found it."

"We found it," Geneva corrected him. "Only Lady V was gone. And now we've found *her.* And here she is! Isn't she beautiful?" She sat the doll up on her lap for the boy to see.

"And that's why we want to see Mrs. Jeffries—to tell her we found Lady V," Ginnie concluded.

Ernie's eyes slid to the doll and away again. He said he had no idea when Mrs. Jeffries would be back. Mrs. Porter thought they had all better go home and have their lunch and take the doll to Miss Wade, leaving a note for Mrs. Jeffries.

Geneva had another idea. "You go home," she told her mother and Mrs. Fellows. "Ginnie and I can wait for Mrs. Jeffries. Maybe she just went to the store or something. And Ernie will take us home in his car. Won't you, Ernie?" She gave him a coaxing smile.

Ernie did not look happy about that. But, Ginnie thought, it won't hurt him. She was getting tired of Ernie's sulks. Why couldn't he be friendly? Without waiting for him to answer, she climbed out of the car. Geneva got out too, with Lady V.

"All right, Ernie?" Mrs. Porter asked.

"Well. . . . Why don't you just leave the doll?"

"No, sir!" Ginnie said. "Nobody is going to steal her again! We're going to take care of Lady V till her owner gets her. Whoever that is," she added with a giggle.

"Oh, by the way, Ernie," Mother said, "would you ask your mother, please, to bring us some new light bulbs? Two of ours have burned out."

Mother and Mrs. Porter left then, with instructions for them to come home when Ernie was ready to leave, whether Mrs. Jeffries had returned or not. Ernie went back up the stairs to the house. Geneva would have followed, but Ginnie said, "I don't think we ought to go in. It's not very polite to make yourself at home in somebody's house when they're away."

So they sat on the steps, Geneva holding the doll. Ginnie leaned forward to gaze at Lady V, and straightened her dress gently. "Ernie acts so cross all the time," Geneva said. "He hates us." She giggled. "I'm glad we're going to get a ride in that funny old car, though."

"I wonder when he's going to get the sports car," Ginnie said.

"When he gets the money, he said."

Ginnie thought about Ernie as they had seen him on the road Saturday, hot and greasy and so humiliated because his old car wouldn't go and they had to give him a lift. He's proud, she thought. He has to do all these jobs and he's poor, but he doesn't want us to be sorry for him. That's why he's cross all the time. Maybe he doesn't really think he'll ever get a sports car. Only he likes cars so much. . . . Suddenly Ginnie made a small strangled sound.

"What's the matter?" Geneva said, looking at her.

"Oh—nothing."

"It was so something. Tell me!"

Ginnie glanced up at the closed door of Mrs. Jeffries' apartment. No, she couldn't be right. Of course she couldn't. But. . . . Then, slowly, she leaned toward Geneva and spoke in a whisper. "Do you think *Ernie* could have taken the car?"

Geneva sat bolt upright. "Ernie wouldn't steal a car!"

"Sh! No, but, well, he likes cars so much." She paused a moment. "I don't really think he took it."

"I should hope not." Geneva paused. "Anyway, he hates dolls, so he certainly didn't take Lady V."

"I didn't think of that." Ginnie gave a sigh of relief.

They sat silent in the pine-scented sunshine, each busy with her thoughts. "I *can't* get over finding her on the beach!" Geneva said.

"Me either." The mystery was too deep for further comment. There was silence again.

Then Geneva said uncertainly, "You don't really think he took the car, do you?"

"I don't know," Ginnie said unhappily.

And then Geneva made up her mind and stood up. "I'm going to ask him."

Ginnie gasped. "He wouldn't tell you!"

"Well, let's see what he says. You take Lady V."

Determinedly Geneva climbed the stairs and knocked on the closed door, while Ginnie's heart thumped against her ribs. Oh, Ernie would be furious! Geneva knocked again, loudly.

This time Ernie opened the door. "What do you want?"

"How soon will you be through?"

"When I get through," he said rudely.

"Well, we want to ask you something."

"I'm busy." He shut the door and after a moment Geneva came back downstairs.

"Geneva, he'll be so mad!" Ginnie said. "Maybe he won't take us home. Don't ask him until we get home. What are you going to *say?*"

"I'll say, 'By the way, did you steal the Jaguar?' " Geneva said mincingly. They both giggled, trying to joke away their nervousness.

But before they had evolved any plan of approach, Ernie emerged. He came down and carried some tools into the garage. In a few moments his car spurted into action and he backed it out. "O.K., let's go," he said.

They climbed in meekly. Ernie shifted, turned the car, and they headed into White Sands Road.

"It seems so funny and high!" Geneva said, making small talk.

Ginnie said nothing. She was trying to think of some way they might approach Ernie, but her thoughts were whirling and she could not collect them. How did you ask someone—someone you liked—if he had stolen a car? And she did like Ernie, in spite of the way he acted. If he'd only be easier to talk to. She stole a look at his face but it was set stonily, his eyes on the road.

It seemed no time at all before they were jouncing along the highway. Now it was hardly any distance home. Ginnie glanced beseechingly at Geneva, and Geneva stirred uncomfortably.

"Ernie," Geneva said.

He made no response.

"Do you—do you like Jaguars?" It was clear that Geneva had lost some of her earlier boldness.

His eyes did not leave the road. "They're O.K."

"Well," Geneva went on, gaining courage, "*somebody* likes them very much, since *somebody* took Mrs. Jeffries' car."

"So?" Ernie said rudely.

Sitting between the two of them, Ginnie began to shiver uncontrollably. Geneva was speaking again. "So it's very mysterious! Because they left the doll on the beach. *Why* would anybody do that?"

"How should I know?" Ernie sounded irritable.

But once started, Geneva was not to be deterred

from her purpose. "Ernie," she said, very softly and gently. Ginnie held her breath. "By any chance did *you* steal the Jaguar?"

The Model A veered, and then Ernie gripped the wheel, pulling it back to the road. "What do you mean—steal! She got it back, didn't she? I just. . . ." He seemed to realize then what he had said. "Why don't you leave me *alone?*" Ernie cried.

Instantly Ginnie felt a rush of compassion. "Oh, Ernie," she said, "we like you! We don't think you'd mean to do anything bad."

"But please help us solve the mystery!" Geneva begged. They had turned off Route 6 and were on the home road now. "Oh, please stop somewhere, Ernie, beside the road, so we can talk just one minute!"

Violently Ernie pulled the car to one side and stepped on the brake so savagely both girls were thrown forward. But he did not look at them. "Now I suppose"—his voice was grim—"you'll tell the cops."

Ginnie was shocked. "Oh, no!" She looked at Geneva.

"Why did you do it?" Geneva demanded. "We won't tell the police if you'll tell us why you took the car."

"Did *you* leave Lady V on the beach?" Ginnie asked, remembering.

There was a long silence while Ernie stared straight ahead. At last he stirred, as if he had made up his mind, and looked down at his thin hands clutching the wheel.

He began to talk. "I went up there yesterday to fix this faucet. She—Mrs. Jeffries—wasn't home, and I could tell there was this party across the way, so I thought she was probably at it. There was the Jag." He paused. "The key was in the ignition. So then I went in and found out I needed another wrench that was at home. I was walking. This crate was out on the Truro Road since Saturday— I hadn't had a chance to get it. So suddenly I thought maybe I could borrow the Jag for five min- utes and run home and get the wrench."

"But. . . ." Ginnie began, puzzled.

He shook his head. "I know. I didn't go home. The minute I got out on the road I knew what a crazy loon I was. My mother would have had a fit.

So I thought, well, since I had the car I'd just run down the road and right back. Boy!" His eyes were dreamy. "Is that Jag smooth!"

"So then," Geneva prompted.

The boy made a curiously helpless gesture. "I don't know what happened. All of a sudden I panicked. I got scared I'd meet the cops or somebody. So I drove down that old road."

"And just *left* it?" Ginnie asked.

"I looked the engine over while I had the chance. Guess I lost track of the time. Then I thought, well, the best thing to do was drive back again, and if she—Mrs. Jeffries—was home, I'd tell her what I did, that's all. But just then—"

"We came along!" Geneva exclaimed.

"I heard somebody coming. I didn't know it was you. So I jumped out and lit off through the woods and down the bluff to the beach. And that's the story."

He turned and faced them for the first time, and it seemed to Ginnie a great load had been lifted from Ernie's conscience.

"But the doll!" Geneva cried. "Why did you take her?"

"Oh. Well, the doll was there. And just as I got out I remembered something you kids said—something about some jewel. So I grabbed her."

Ginnie drew a deep breath. The jewel *was* mixed up in it. "Did you find any jewel?"

"No."

She let her breath out. Of course there was no jewel.

"So you left her on the beach!" Geneva said accusingly. "She could have been ruined!"

Again Ernie turned to look at them. "Think I was going to walk home carrying a doll? You want to know something? I was down there today. I was going to get her and put her in my own car and slip her back to Mrs. Jeffries. But you kids came along. So I put the doll where you couldn't help but see her!"

Ginnie heard Geneva gasp. "You were that noise!"

All three were silent as part of the puzzle, at least, lay assembled before them at last.

Ernie moved abruptly then, and the motor sprang to life. No one spoke as they drove on down the road and turned into the driveway. He stopped the car.

"Then," Ginnie said slowly, as both girls sat there, not moving yet to get out, "you didn't *really* steal the car—or the doll—because. . . ." She hesitated, wanting to put the unhappy escapade in the best light for Ernie.

But Ernie was speaking, and when he turned toward her, Ginnie saw that his face was strained and white and the bones showed through.

"You're right. I didn't really steal the doll," Ernie said in a queer, flat, even voice, "because—do you want to know something?—that doll just happens to be *my property!*"

His tone changed. "Get out now, I'm in a hurry."

Speechless, they climbed out. Ernie backed his Model A quickly down the drive, turned, and was gone.

CHAPTER 10

The Answer

"LADY V!" said Miss Wade softly. She took the doll from Geneva's hands. "You've come home!"

They were on the screened porch—the two girls and their mothers and Miss Wade. Ginnie's head was whirling. Her excitement over finding the doll and solving the mystery of the stolen car had been pushed into the background by Ernie's astounding announcement—"That doll just happens to be *my property*."

Ginnie and Geneva had had no time to discuss what he had meant by this strange statement. Should they tell Miss Wade? Ernie had confided in them.

But there was one thing, now, that they could ask her. "Geneva," Ginnie said impulsively, "let's ask Miss Wade about—you know, in the diary."

"O.K."

Ginnie began. "In that old diary of your mother's we read something mysterious. Wait." She paused. "Can I get the diary?"

"It's on the parlor table."

Ginnie ran in and came back with the slim old volume. "Now, if I can find it. . . ." She leafed through the pages slowly, coming at last to the sentences she wanted. "Here! Listen." She read, *"My dolly, that Uncle Frank brought me from Paris, has a precious jewel. But sh! It's a secret!"*

They all looked at Miss Wade, and there was silence for a minute. Then Miss Wade gave a little sigh and smiled at them.

"Yes," she said.

"Was there a precious jewel?" Geneva cried.

"There was a pearl. Not a regular pearl—a conch pearl. Uncle Frank brought it to my mother from the West Indies. She hung it around Lady V's neck on a silk thread and pretended it was a precious jewel."

"Wasn't it?" Ginnie asked wistfully. Not that she had really believed in a precious jewel.

"No, not really."

"What is a conch pearl exactly?" Mother asked.

"It came from . . . why, from that shell right there!" Miss Wade turned to look at the great pink conch in the door to the kitchen. "Uncle Frank brought the shell, too, as a souvenir. But conch pearls aren't valuable, like pearls from oysters."

Ginnie gazed at the graceful shell she had held to her ear so often. So this, at last, was the story of the precious jewel.

"What happened to it?" Geneva asked.

Miss Wade looked down at the doll in her lap, then at the girls again. "It was on Lady V when she—disappeared. It isn't on her now." She smiled, a little ruefully. "I've never mentioned that pearl to a soul in all these years," she said suddenly. "I've always been so ashamed to think I left Lady V and the pearl lying around for someone to pick up! My mother treasured it."

"Didn't you ever try to get the doll back?" Mother asked.

"I never thought of Lady V till months after the Lamberts had gone," Miss Wade said. "Then I hated to have any unpleasantness. After all, the value was only sentimental. Though I did hate to think they had taken her."

Tires crunched on gravel then as a car turned into the driveway next door. "There's Mrs. Evans," Mother said. "She must be bringing those light bulbs. We're over here, Mrs. Evans," she called.

Ernie's mother came across the grass. "Come in, Martha," Miss Wade said, and Ginnie got up to open the screen door.

"Good afternoon," Mrs. Evans said pleasantly. She glanced around at the group, then at the doll on Miss Wade's lap. "Why!" Mrs. Evans cried, delight in her voice. "You've got Lady Vanderbilt!"

For a moment no one spoke, and Ginnie felt a strange sense of confusion. Then Mother said quickly to Miss Wade, "Does Mrs. Evans know the story?"

"No," Miss Wade said. "Martha—you've seen this doll before?"

"Seen her before!" Mrs. Evans laughed. "She's my doll!"

They all stared. "But—but," Geneva stammered, "she was at the auction!"

"I gave her to the auction. Mrs. French asked if I had anything they could auction off. I didn't have a thing but some old buttons. I gave her those. Then I thought about Lady V and, well, I just loved her but I thought maybe she'd bring some money for the church. Goodness knows I haven't much to give." She looked from one to the other. "Did one of you buy her?"

They all looked at Miss Wade. And slowly Miss Wade spoke. "No, Martha, somebody else did. But—I must tell you. Lady Vanderbilt was my mother's doll. She disappeared from my attic thirty years ago, and I never saw her again until today."

A change came over Mrs. Evans. The happy light that had come into her eyes at the discovery of the doll faded. After a moment she said in a low voice, "I never knew she was yours." She and Miss Wade looked at one another. "Ma brought her home," Mrs. Evans said.

"Sarah!" Miss Wade sounded unbelieving.

"And all these years I've thought the Lamberts. . . .
I can't believe it!"

Mrs. Evans spoke quickly. "She didn't steal her,
Miss Wade! She brought her home and she was
very mad. She said the children in a house where
she worked were going to ruin the doll. So she
brought her home for safekeeping. But she didn't
tell me who she belonged to. I was just a little tyke.
She only told me her name was Lady Vanderbilt
and we must take very good care of her. But Ma
died before you got home from Europe. Remember, Miss Wade?"

"I remember," Miss Wade said quietly.

"And I did take good care of her, didn't I?" Mrs.
Evans was eager. "I kept her clothes real good.
And I only gave her to the auction because I didn't
have any girl to hand her on to."

Now we know, Ginnie thought. All of a sudden
we know where Lady V was. But there was one
more thing. She was, naturally, the first to think
of it.

"Miss Wade," she said, "the pearl."

"Do you remember, Martha," Miss Wade asked,

"whether the doll had a necklace when you first saw her? A pearl?"

Mrs. Evans' brow furrowed. "No, I don't remember any pearl."

"What happened to the doll after your mother died?" Mrs. Porter asked.

"She stayed in the house until my dad died. I was married then and when I cleared out the house to sell it I took Lady V home. She never had any pearl that I can recall."

"Don't worry about it," Miss Wade said. She stood up. "Martha, you don't know what a mystery you've solved. These children have been sleuthing around here for weeks, trying to find the answer to Lady V's whereabouts. And all the time. . . ." She shook her head. "I can't believe it yet!"

Suddenly Ginnie gave a small gasp. She clapped her hands over her mouth and met Geneva's eyes. That was why Ernie said the doll was his property. He had told the truth, too, when he said he had found no jewel.

Mrs. Evans, still troubled, took her leave. Mrs.

Porter looked at her wrist watch. "Do you people realize it's way past lunch time? What do you say we all go out and get a lobster roll somewhere?"

"Yes!" Geneva cried.

"Will you join us, Miss Wade?" Mother asked.

Miss Wade thanked them and declined. "Well, anyway," Ginnie said, "Lady V is back in her old home! I hope Mrs. Jeffries will give her to you."

"We'll see." Miss Wade smiled at them. "Have fun now."

Blue skies smiled and sunlight danced to match Ginnie's soaring spirits. They had solved the mystery that had plagued them for days. They took the road across the moors, and headed for Provincetown. Sun-drenched fields of bay and brilliant beach plums followed the cool shade of the pines. Climbing, dipping, curving under the open sky, the road gave view after view of shimmering water and low green rolling hills. From North Truro they followed the shore to the teeming little town of the Pilgrims' first landing.

Munching a lobster roll and gazing over the water, Ginnie felt completely happy. Daddy will be here Saturday to stay the rest of the summer, she thought. What a lot of things I have to tell him!

They had parked the car in the big lot near the Pilgrim Monument and walked down through the narrow streets crowded with slow-moving cars. After lunch the girls poked into gift shops.

Mother and Mrs. Porter had stopped in an antique shop. Geneva saw the sign of the Province-town Playhouse, and she and Ginnie wandered out on the wharf behind the famous old theater. Young men were painting stage scenery laid flat on the wharf. The girls watched for a few minutes, and looked through the open doors of the shabby little playhouse, where a woman idly dusted stage furniture.

It was Ginnie who saw Mrs. Jeffries. Mrs. Jeffries had an easel set up on the beach beside the wharf and she was painting.

They were upon her. "Mrs. Jeffries!" Ginnie cried.

"We found the doll!" Geneva shouted.

Brush suspended, she gazed at them. "You *did?*"

"On the beach." Geneva was breathless. "And oh, we've got the most wonderful, exciting things to tell you!"

"I'm dying to hear." Mrs. Jeffries glanced quickly at the sky. "Look, honey, I want to hear, but I've got to catch this light while it lasts. I'll be home late tonight and I'll see you tomorrow. Where can I find you?"

Ginnie told her where they were staying.

"O.K. I'll see you in the morning. 'By now!"

Mrs. Jeffries turned away, instantly absorbed in her painting again.

In the morning she came. The girls were watching and went bounding across the lawn to meet her. Then the three of them went over to Miss Wade's house.

"Good morning to you all," Miss Wade said, opening the door.

For a moment Mrs. Jeffries stood on the porch looking around. Ginnie saw her eyes wander into the kitchen, then rest on the conch shell. Lady Vanderbilt was seated in a rocker, and slowly Mrs. Jeffries picked her up. "So here you are! I simply can't wait to hear the story."

They told her first about finding the doll on the beach, enjoying her amazement. "But why on earth would anybody abandon this doll on the beach?" she exclaimed.

"That old road must run along the water at that point," Miss Wade said. "It's not far from where you found the car down to the beach."

"But I still don't understand. . . ."

"Well," Geneva said with satisfaction, "we'll begin at the beginning and tell you the whole story." She looked at Ginnie. "Shall we tell about —you know?"

Suddenly Ginnie saw that they had to tell about Ernie's part. If they did not, if the police kept working on the theft of the car, Ernie might be in real trouble. They would have to trust Mrs. Jeffries and Miss Wade. She nodded gravely to Geneva, and they began.

"Lady Vanderbilt—that's the doll's name—was Miss Wade's mother's doll," Ginnie said. "Only many years ago she disappeared from the attic when some people rented the house."

"And we just found out where she was," Geneva went on. She related yesterday's discovery. "And then Mrs. Evans decided she would give Lady V for the auction because she didn't have any girl. And you bought her!"

"And we were there!" Geneva reminded them all.

Mrs. Jeffries spoke slowly. "What a strange story." There was an odd expression, Ginnie thought, in her eyes. "But—the car. And the doll's being left on the beach. They had no connection with this story, surely."

"Yes!" Geneva cried.

Ginnie saw the startled look on Miss Wade's face and she spoke quickly. "But Mrs. Jeffries, we have to ask you a big, big favor." She glanced at Miss Wade. "You don't know about this either, Miss Wade."

"No, I certainly do not."

"We know who took the car," Geneva said. Both women looked at her, waiting.

"And he didn't mean to steal it." Ginnie picked up the story. "He just needed a wrench he'd left at home, and the key was in the car, and he likes cars so much. . . ."

"Ernie!" Miss Wade said in a low voice.

"Yes," Ginnie said. "That's who it was. Ernie." Quickly, between them, she and Geneva filled in the story.

"So please, Mrs. Jeffries, don't tell the police!" Ginnie begged. "Ernie didn't mean to do anything bad."

Mrs. Jeffries looked at Miss Wade. "He's a good boy," Miss Wade said slowly. "I don't think he'll do a thing like this again."

"All right." Mrs. Jeffries flashed a smile at the

girls. "This will be our secret." Suddenly she said, "Miss Wade, I've had the most curious feeling ever since I got to your house. Would you mind—could I go inside a minute?"

"Come in!"

The girls followed. Mrs. Jeffries gazed around the kitchen. She walked slowly into the dining room and parlor. The girls saw her eyes rest on the organ, move to the stairs. "May I go up?"

She did not go beyond the upper hall. She stood for a minute, gazing up at the trap door to the attic. Then she faced Miss Wade, suppressed excitement in her face.

"I was right!" she said. "Do you know who I am?"

They all stared at her.

"I lived in this house that summer your doll disappeared. I am the little Lambert girl!"

CHAPTER 11

Pretty Thing

GINNIE drew a sudden breath. She was conscious that Geneva had her mouth open.

"Let me sit down," Miss Wade was saying. She sat down on an old sofa, looking up at Mrs. Jeffries.

"When I saw that doll at the auction," Mrs. Jeffries said, "it stirred such a memory that I had to buy her. But I didn't realize she was actually the same doll! You see, my brother—he was older; I was only four—my brother got the ladder one day and we climbed up to the attic. We found the doll. All I remember is holding her and thinking she was the most beautiful doll I had ever seen. Then someone—that must have been your Sarah—came up and took the doll away. But I never forgot her."

"But didn't you remember that you stayed in Miss Wade's house?" Ginnie asked, puzzled.

"I just knew we stayed in some house around here. I've never been on the Cape since. I'm a Californian, you know. I came east to college and then to live when I got married. When I knew I was coming up here, I wrote my mother, but she couldn't recall Miss Wade's name. But when I drove in this morning. . . . I can't get over it!"

But there was still, Ginnie recalled again, that one unanswered question. She hated to ask it one more time, it seemed so stubborn and foolish. Still, she had to be absolutely sure. And after this she would forget it. "Mrs. Jeffries"—she looked up at the young woman—"do you remember . . . I don't think you would, but by any chance do you remember . . . whether Lady V had a necklace on?"

"Oh, *Ginnie!*" Geneva sounded impatient.

Mrs. Jeffries thought. "No, I don't." She looked from one to the other. "What sort of necklace was it?"

"A pearl," Ginnie told her, "on a silk thread."

"But not really a pearl, not an oyster pearl," Miss Wade put in. "It was a conch pearl, Mrs.

Jeffries, so don't be concerned. It's disappeared somewhere during these years, but the value was only sentimental, so I've forgotten it." She made a gesture of dismissal.

"You say it was a conch pearl?" Mrs. Jeffries was looking at her. "What did it look like?"

"Oh, it had rather a pretty shape. A sort of tear-drop, fairly large, pale pink. . . ."

"Wait a minute!" They all turned at the excitement in Mrs. Jeffries' voice. "Yes, yes, she did have it on! I remember the feel! It was smooth like— like ivory. . . ."

Ginnie sat where she had dropped cross-legged on the floor. Something she could not quite get hold of was struggling to the surface of her consciousness. Smooth . . . like ivory. Pink. Where. . . .

Then she knew. For a moment she sat perfectly still, then, trying to be quite calm, she got to her feet. "I'll be right back."

Once out of the house, she flew across the lawn. Mother and Mrs. Porter were out. Up the stairs to her bedroom she raced.

The jar was on her bureau. Heart beating fast,

Ginnie unscrewed the cover, poured buttons on her bed. Eyes and fingers feverishly searched. Then she picked it out of the heap.

Under the dirt surely it was pink. And smooth, like ivory, shaped like a teardrop.

"I can't bear it, I can't bear it!" Ginnie said out loud. "Oh, it can't be!"

She dashed back across the lawn, up the stairs. They looked at her curiously. "What happened?" Geneva asked.

Ginnie held it clutched tight. She looked up at Miss Wade. "I know this couldn't be it," she said. "I'm silly, I know I'm silly." She opened her hand, extending the palm to Miss Wade.

Both women bent to look. Geneva scrambled up. And then it was in Miss Wade's hand and she was staring down, unbelieving.

"This is Lady Vanderbilt's pearl," Miss Wade said.

Afterward they figured it out. "Sarah must have put it away for safekeeping," Miss Wade said. "It got in with her buttons."

"And Mrs. Evans gave those old buttons to the auction," Ginnie concluded.

They had solved the mystery—every bit of the mystery. "I'm going to tell Mother!" Geneva cried.

"I've got to run along too," Mrs. Jeffries said. "I've never been in such a whirl in my life!"

On the porch the artist stood looking at Lady

Vanderbilt. "She looks so serene. Miss Wade, I want you to keep her."

"I would be so grateful to have her back!" Miss Wade said.

Her hand on the screen door, Mrs. Jeffries paused. "We ought to celebrate. We've got to have a party, and talk and talk. Could you all come to tea Saturday?"

"Our fathers are coming Saturday," Geneva told her.

"Good. Bring Miss Wade and your mothers and fathers."

There was a car at Mrs. Jeffries' house when they drove into the clearing on Saturday. Mother and Daddy and Miss Wade were in one car; the Porters, Ginnie and Geneva—and Lady V—were in the other.

When they climbed the stairs to where Mrs. Jeffries waited, Dr. Emerson rose to greet them.

"You know my darling Professor Emerson," Mrs. Jeffries said. "He had a part in this, since you found me through him. But I haven't told him the story."

Professor Emerson shook hands. "I understand a first-rate thriller of a mystery is about to be unfolded."

"But wait till we've had tea," Mrs. Jeffries instructed. "Talk about unimportant things while I'm in the kitchen!"

Ginnie and Geneva carried plates of thin bread and butter and marmalade and little cakes. There was lemonade for them. Mrs. Jeffries poured the tea and the girls passed sugar and cream and lemon. And there was pleasant conversation.

At last their hostess put down her cup. "Now! I can't wait another minute to tell Professor Emerson our story. Why don't you begin, Miss Wade? Then Ginnie and Geneva can tell about the auction."

They told the story, first Miss Wade, then the girls. Now it was Mrs. Jeffries' turn, beginning with seeing the doll at the auction and ending with the strange experience of recognizing Miss Wade's house.

There was not a word about Ernie, though. Ginnie had told Mother and probably Mother had told Daddy. But they skipped that part now.

Ginnie related the grand climax—her sudden hunch that she might have the conch pearl in her possession.

"So that is the mystery of the missing doll," Daddy said.

"And quite a story." Dr. Emerson nodded slowly. "Really quite remarkable." He leaned forward to knock the ashes from his pipe. "No clue to who took the car and abandoned the lady doll?" Ginnie glanced at him quickly, but Dr. Emerson answered his own question. "No, I assume not." He cleared his throat. "I'd like to see that conch pearl."

"I've got it right here." Miss Wade reached for her bag.

They clustered about. "I washed it," Miss Wade said. "See what a lovely luster it has, even after all these years."

"May I look at it?" The professor took it from her hand.

"It's a pretty thing," Mother said. "Miss Wade, you'll have to wear it."

"You could put it on a gold chain," Geneva suggested.

Dr. Emerson was speaking. "But this," he said, and he turned the pearl in his hand, "this is a particularly fine specimen of a conch pearl."

Miss Wade looked surprised. "Oh?"

"Occasionally they are very valuable, you know, depending on shape, largely, and size and luster."

"Well, I would be very happy if it had any value," Miss Wade said. She hesitated, gazing at the pearl doubtfully. "Do you really think—would it be worthwhile to have an expert. . . ."

"Dr. Emerson is by way of being an expert himself," Mrs. Jeffries said. "Marine biology was his special line."

"Conchology is rather in my field," Dr. Emerson admitted. "I couldn't estimate the value. But unless I'm very wrong"—he eyed the pearl again—"and I don't think I am, you have a pearl here that is worth a great deal of money."

"Oh, Miss Wade," Geneva gasped, "you can have a new roof!"

They all laughed then, breaking the tension, and Miss Wade said, "I—I can't quite take this in. I don't need much money, of course. Just enough. . . ."

"There should be more than enough—much more," Dr. Emerson said quietly. He laid the pearl on the table, where they could all admire it. "But I suggest you get this gem into your safe-deposit box first thing Monday, Miss Wade. Then, if you like, I can suggest someone to appraise it."

"Please don't let it get lost again!" Ginnie begged.

Mrs. Jeffries jumped up. "That reminds me! I have something for you, Miss Wade." She went into the bedroom and returned with a canvas. "I added the pearl to Lady Vanderbilt's portrait. May I present the painting to you with the compliments of the artist?" She turned the picture of the doll so they could all see it.

Miss Wade exclaimed, "How perfectly wonderful! What a beautiful portrait! You don't know, my dear, what this means to me. Because I've decided to give Lady V to the Historical Society. She'll have a good home there and nobody can ever whisk her away again."

Ginnie said suddenly, "Miss Wade, do you think your mother knew it was really a precious jewel? She said so in the diary."

"I know she didn't," Miss Wade replied. "She loved it because Uncle Frank gave it to her. The pearl was precious to her. Uncle Frank. . . ." She paused, thoughtful.

"Did he know?" Geneva asked.

"Uncle Frank was a queer one, I always heard. He had no children and my mother was his favorite niece. I just don't know," Miss Wade said.

They all talked then, excitedly, about the picture and the pearl and the mystery. Only Miss Wade sat quiet. It was during a lull that Mrs. Jeffries said, "Miss Wade, a penny for those thoughts!"

"Oh!" The older woman started. "I'm sorry! I was woolgathering."

She paused. "Ernie Evans," she said, and she looked from Ginnie to Geneva to Mrs. Jeffries. The good professor was suddenly very busy with his pipe. "He's never had a thing, that boy. And he's a *good* boy. If that pearl is really worth anything, I'd like to help Ernie somehow."

They were thoughtful for a moment. Then Geneva remarked, "Dr. Emerson said Ernie wants to go to college."

"Yes," Miss Wade said. "Well"—and she smiled suddenly at them all—"we'll see."

It was Ginnie who jumped up, to cross the room and kiss Miss Wade gently on the cheek.

CATHERINE WOOLLEY was born in Chicago but has lived all her life in Passaic, New Jersey, where she is well known for her community activities. A former member of the Passaic Board of Education, she is active on local citizens' committees. She has served on the Passaic Redevelopment Agency, is a member of the board of directors and past president of the League of Women Voters of Passaic, a member of the Red Cross Motor Corps, and on the board of directors of the Passaic-Clifton branch of the American Association for the United Nations. Miss Woolley owns an old house on Cape Cod, and she spends several months there every year.

After graduating from the University of California at Los Angeles, she returned to New York City, where she was in advertising, sales promotion, and editorial work until 1947. Her interest in her own young nephews and nieces drew her to the field of writing for children, and *Two Hundred Pennies,* her first book published by William Morrow and Company, appeared in 1947. Since then Catherine Woolley has become widely known for her stories for the eight-to-twelve age group, and in addition has gained a large and enthusiastic younger following for her picture books, for which she uses the pen name of Jane Thayer.